The

ISLAND

of

BOOKS

DOMINIQUE FORTIER

translated by RHONDA MULLINS

COACH HOUSE BOOKS, TORONTO

First English edition. Originally published in French in 2015 as
Au péril de la mer by Les Éditions Alto.

Coach House Books acknowledges the financial support of the Government of Canada through the National Translation Program for Book Publishing, an initiative of the Roadmap for Canada's Official Languages 2013-2018: Education, Immigration, Communities, for our translation activities. We also thank the Canada Council for the Arts and the Ontario Arts Council for their generous assistance. We further acknowledge the support of the Government of Canada through the Canada Book Fund.

LIBRARY AND ARCHIVES CANADA CATALOGUING IN PUBLICATION

Fortier, Dominique, 1972-
[Au péril de la mer. English]
    The island of books / by Dominique Fortier ; translated by
    Rhonda Mullins.

Translation of: Au péril de la mer.
ISBN 978-1-55245-338-4

    I. Mullins, Rhonda, 1966-, translator II. Title. III. Title: Au
péril de la mer. English

PS8611.O7733A913 2016   C843'.6   C2016-904388-6

The Island of Books is available as an ebook: ISBN 978 1 77056 471 8 (EPUB), ISBN 978 1 77056 472 5 (PDF), ISBN 978 1 77056 473 2 (MOBI)

Purchase of the print version of this book entitles you to a free digital copy. To claim your ebook of this title, please email sales@ chbooks.com with proof of purchase or visit chbooks.com/digital. (Coach House Books reserves the right to terminate the free digital download offer at any time.)

For Fred, and Zoé.

The first time I saw it I was thirteen years old, that limbo of an age between childhood and adolescence when you already know who you are but don't yet know if that's who you will ever be. It was like love at first sight. I don't remember anything very specific, aside from a certainty, a wonder so deep it was like a stupor: I had found the place I had always been looking for, without realizing it, without even knowing it existed.

Twenty-five years would pass before I would see it again. When the time came to return, I suggested that we not go: we didn't have much time before we had to head back to Paris; they were calling for rain; it would probably be crawling with tourists. In truth, I was afraid, the way you're afraid any time you go back to the places of your childhood, afraid of finding them diminished, which means one of two things: either they appeared larger because your eyes were so small, or along the way you lost the knack for wonder, either of which is a devastating idea. But it hadn't changed, and neither had I.

§

No matter what angle you look at it from, you can't see exactly where the rock ends and the church begins. It's as if the mountain itself is narrowing, stretching, tapering to a point – without human intervention – to give the abbey its shape. It's as if the rock one morning decided to climb toward the heavens, stopping one thousand years later. But it didn't always look the way it does today: the familiar silhouette that has been captured in countless photographs, topped by the spire on which the archangel dances, dates only from the nineteenth century.

Before the seventh century, Mont Saint-Michel didn't even exist; the rocky isle where the abbey stands today was known as Mont Tombe – a mountain twice over, because it seems that the word *tombe* didn't mean a tomb or a grave, but a simple knoll.

Around the sixth century, two hermits living on Mont Tombe erected two small chapels, one dedicated to Saint Stephen (the first Christian martyr) and the other to Saint Symphorian (to whom we owe the strange and illuminating phrase, uttered as he was being tortured, *The world passes like a shadow*). They lived in complete isolation, devoting their days to prayer and their nights to holy visions. They lived with nothing: each one had a cowl, a coat and a blanket, and they had one knife between them. When they were short on food, they would light a fire of wet moss and grass; from the shore, residents would see the smoke and load up a donkey with food, and the beast would travel the island's road alone to deliver supplies to the holy men, who did not want to sully themselves with human contact. The men would unload the provisions a bit reluctantly; they would have preferred to need only their faith to sustain them. The donkey would return along the same path, empty baskets slapping against its flanks, its step light in the sand of the bay.

Legend, or a variation on the legend, has it that one day the donkey ran into a wolf, which devoured it. From that day on, the wolf brought food to the hermits.

§

During my daughter's first summer, we would go for a walk every morning. After a few minutes, she would nod off in her stroller, and I would stop at Joyce Park or Pratt Park to watch the ducks. It was a moment of peace, often the only one in the day. I would sit on a bench in the shade of a tree, pull a small Moleskine and a felt pen from the bag on the stroller, and as if in a dream I would follow the man who more than five centuries ago lived among the rocks of Mont Saint-Michel. His story would mix with the squawking of the ducklings, the wind blowing through the two ginkgos, male and female, the squirrels racing through the towering catalpa with leaves broad as faces, and the fluttering eyelids of my daughter, who had surrendered to sleep. I would jot all this down haphazardly on the page because it seemed to me that these moments were important and that unless they were recorded, they would slip from my grasp forever. My notebook was half novel, half field notes, an aide-mémoire.

In the evening, I often didn't have the energy to bring in the stroller before going to bed. One night, there was a big storm that soaked everything. In the morning, the notebook had doubled in volume and looked like a water-soaked sponge. Its pages were crinkled, and half the words had disappeared – specifically, the middle half: the right half of the left-hand pages and the left half of the right-hand pages. The rest could still be read clearly, but halfway along each line the words became blurred, faded, washed out to the point of disappearing. That may be how, with their ink running together, my story ended up merging with the story of Mont Saint-Michel. I couldn't unravel them.

This anecdote is a lot like the final scene in *On the Proper Use of Stars*, in which Lady Jane knocks her cup of tea over the maps she has spent hours drawing, the colours running as she watches. If I had invented it, I would have written it differently. But there you have it, every day words drown in the rain, tears, tea, stories get tangled up, the past and the present come together, the rocks and the trees talk to each other above our heads.

How these 2 men who
never existed but whom I try
To invent at same time
nt where they live
will they do to
reach the shore
Pratt Park
I know they
to write
I dreamed that night that the abbey
was drifting on
a stormy sea, brushing against
riding out waves as high as

§

In the year of our Lord 14**, Mont Saint-Michel towered in
the middle of the bay; the abbey stood tall at its centre. In
the middle of the abbey, the church was nestled around its
choir. A man was lying in the middle of the transept. The
heart of this man held a sorrow so deep that the bay wasn't
enough to contain it.

He didn't have faith, but the church didn't hold that
against him. There is suffering so great that it exempts you
from believing. Sprawled on the flagstones, arms spread
wide, Éloi was himself a cross.

At certain hours, the abbey is silent and the rooms deserted. Between matins and lauds, a blue light descends, time stops to catch its breath. This hour is not for ordinary mortals, snoring quietly: it belongs to the sick, the insane and the lovers. It is the hour when I would wake up at Anna's side as she dozed, to listen to her light breath. She would sleep in the most unlikely positions: arms folded, legs crossed, as if sleep were amusing itself by having her pose for me in her dreams. Through the window, I would see the sea-blue sky grow darker again. A few minutes later it would grow brighter and day would begin for everyone, but this moment belonged to me.

I still wake up at that nebulous hour between night and day, and, over a year later, I still reach for her sleeping body near mine. Every time, it takes me a few seconds to recall the simple fact: she is no longer. I lose her again every morning before sunrise. One would think that feeling the same pain over and over every day would help it subside, like the blade of a knife losing its bite as it slices further into flesh, but that's not what happens. Every day, I lose her for the first time. She never stops dying.

I am not a man of God, I am not a man of science. I was an artist and I am no longer. The little that I know of the world, I owe to accounts of those more learned than me. Here is what I know: I loved a woman and she is dead.

The woman in question was not mine. She was married to another, but she belonged to no one. She had jet-black hair and eyes of a colour I have never seen anywhere else, neither before nor since. Now she is in the ground, being eaten by worms. Robert answers grudgingly when I ask him where the dead dwell. I would like to believe, as he does, that she is with God the Father in his kingdom, surrounded by the just. I don't know how to reconcile these two ideas.

Is it possible that the kingdom of God is overrun with worms and that everyone just fumbles along, disfigured, eye sockets hollow? These questions are beyond me, and I try not to think about them, but they come to haunt me in my dreams. And then lauds is rung, the monks get up and head in a long line to the chapel, where they sing the dawn of the new day.

She was the daughter of a rich merchant, and I was the son of no one at all.

I have a middling talent as a painter: I apprenticed at an atelier where I was first assigned to filling in background landscapes on which those more seasoned sketched portraits of the rich and powerful, and then later I was allowed to create their likenesses. After a few years, I had built a large enough clientele to leave the atelier and receive buyers at my home. I quickly understood the advantage of giving the bourgeois the nobility that was lacking in their faces. They found themselves more pleasing in my paintings than in their mirrors, blamed the mirrors, and came back to see me when they wanted a portrait of their wives or mistresses.

I soon acquired a reputation, and it had become good form for notables to have their portrait painted by Éloi Leroux. I say this without vanity: the town had few portrait artists and none who worked as quickly as I did, so I was never short of commissions. For a while I could even afford the luxury of turning down work. Of the work I was offered, I preferred the sort that paid well and that gave me an opportunity for amusement. I had long since stopped painting notaries and bishops in their depressing robes. For pleasure, I instead did sketches of birds – in flight, pecking, building their nests or feeding their young. I liked their colours, and the fact that they didn't stay still. I particularly liked that they were absolutely indifferent to my presence. I started drawing eggs, which gave me respite from the rest of it.

One particular week I had agreed, as a favour to a friend who in turn owed a favour to her family, to do the portrait of a young girl who was getting married. I had nevertheless taken pains to inquire as to whether she was pretty.

'I don't know,' my friend replied. 'But I know she is young.'

'Well, that's something at least,' I answered, imagining one of those pale damsels whose likeness needed to be captured once it had been decided she would be given to a seigneur who was far away and far from convinced, and who wanted to get a look before committing.

The morning of the first sitting, as I was running my hand over a panel of poplar to make sure there were no splinters or slivers, I was already preparing to even out a ruddy complexion, soften the line of the chin or trim a long nose, and then she walked in, escorted by a governess. Out of the corner of my eye, I saw that she was thin and dark-haired, but I didn't turn right away, letting her examine the sheet she was to sit in front of, which depicted a roughly sketched winding country road. Over the years, I had noticed that people who were about to be captured in paint almost always felt awkward. In their embarrassment, they revealed something that they then tried to hide from me during the long hours of sitting and that in spite of them found its way into their portraits. The discomfort that made them unintentionally reveal something was like the background of the painting, invisible but there, and it coloured the rest. But when I finally turned, she was leaning on the faldstool I had set out for her, studying me calmly. Still today, I could not tell you what colour her eyes were. In my shock, I dropped the brush and, in moving to catch it, knocked over a bowl of water.

'Don't be nervous. It'll be fine,' she said, smiling a little.

If my life had depended on it, I would not have been able to say in that moment whether she was sincerely trying to put me at ease or mocking me.

The first day, I did only the shape of her face: drawn straight-on; three-quarters; bathed in the midday light streaming in through the window; in profile; curtains half-drawn, in the light of a candle that left part in shadow.

The second day, I drew the simple hairstyle that held back her black curls, sketched her high forehead and the arch of her eyebrows on her pale skin. The third day I spent sitting, watching her and examining my still virtually untouched wood panel, as if to measure the distance between one and the other. I drew closer to her, I held out my hand to arrange a strand of hair, but the governess stopped me and tucked the wayward curl behind her ear, while Anna remained immobile, staring straight ahead. The fourth day, I had to explain to her that it would take me at least another week to complete the portrait. As I said the words, I thought: one month, at the very least one month, maybe two.

'You realize you won't be paid any more,' pointed out my friend, who had come at the family's request to see how the portrait was progressing.

He seemed a little worried about the turn events were taking. I clicked my tongue to let him know it was of no importance.

She would arrive at my atelier mid-morning every day and stay until the light began to fade. The entire time, she remained seated, as still as a statue, a trace of a smile on her lips and in her eyes. She watched me with quiet curiosity, asking no questions. The first few days, she would not speak either, and all that could be heard in the room was the *whish* of the brush on the wood panel and the loud breathing of the governess.

When she left, I would remain seated in front of the unfinished painting, unable to leave her. The idea that she would stop coming to my atelier in a few days had become unbearable, as if I had been told that I would now have to live without the sun or my hands. I found comfort in the painting, which was like an imperfect little sister to her. But I would have to give up the portrait as well.

One evening, I set a second easel beside the one that held the painting I was working on. On this second easel I placed a smaller oak panel, which, when I ran my fingers over it, was as soft as a woman's cheek. In the half-light, I started to paint a second Anna on it, drawn half from the first portrait and half from my imagination.

The face was a pale mask, framed by loose hair floating in dark waves. Lips slightly parted (had I ever seen her teeth?), forming a pout I had invented for her, between smile and malice. For the eyes, I mixed my most precious powders to create a thick, almost colourless paste, which, lacking anything better, I spread so thinly on the silver leaf that there was still a muted shine under the egg tempera.

The two portraits were progressing at approximately the same pace; unlike Penelope, who, in the night, undid the work accomplished during the day, I used the first one as a guide to finish the second piece, devoting to it all the hours from sundown to sun-up. Wracked with fatigue, I would fall asleep at the first glimmer of dawn. Before Anna arrived, I would make sure I hid any evidence of this nighttime portrait, but one morning my exhaustion got the better of me. I collapsed fully dressed on a pile of blankets that I had thrown in a corner, and I dreamed of dunes slowly engulfed by the sea.

When I awoke, she was standing in front of the second portrait. Seeing them side by side like that, my first thought was that my painting did not do her justice, and my heart clenched. But then I realized I would never see her again, and the tightness in my chest became a fist.

As I rose and tried to straighten my clothing and my hair to compose myself, she turned to me and said in a clear voice, pointing to the smaller of the two portraits, 'I want that one.'

I mustered the courage to answer, with a hoarse voice, 'I doubt it would please your future husband,' but before reaching my lips, the words *future husband* became a ball of thorns in my throat.

From that day on, we started to have unwieldy triangular conversations, the governess serving as an interpreter, as if we weren't speaking the same language.

'Is this the first time you have had your portrait painted?' I asked her, not finding anything more interesting to say.

She didn't answer, or did so by shrugging her shoulders, almost imperceptibly. The woman in black started talking.

'Great artists have captured Mademoiselle's likeness, names you are no doubt familiar with, such as...'

In a haughty tone, she listed some of the most celebrated portrait artists in the county.

'The first portrait was painted when Mademoiselle was just one year old. It was so perfect that her father long refused to part with it, and he took it with him when he travelled. A number of others were painted over the years. The most recent was last summer.'

'No doubt it is also a masterpiece. But then, tell me, why call on my services this time?'

The governess opened her mouth and closed it immediately, as if suddenly realizing that there was no answer to that question. She glanced quickly at Anna.

'Perhaps Mademoiselle had seen my portraits?' I ventured, pride getting the better of me.

The governess gave a sharp nod to indicate that that was a plausible theory.

A few months later, when she was lying by my side, her hair tousled, and I was tracing the line of her jaw with my thumb, Anna told me, a trace of pink on her lily-white cheeks, 'I had never seen your portraits, but I had seen you.'

Perhaps I should have been insulted, but I rejoiced like a child at this confession.

§

I was awakened one night by light on my eyelids. I opened my eyes: the moon was practically full behind a veil of clouds, and a white light fell across my face. I looked around at the monks sleeping. They had gone to bed right after compline and were sleeping like the dead. Snoring had begun, resonant, regular. At the other end of the room, someone was quietly whimpering. Whether he was suffering in a dream or trying to give himself pleasure, I didn't know, nor did I know why it is that men have only one noise for both pleasure and pain.

Some monks had their own cell, but I slept in a room with sixteen others. It was like bees in a hive, and then I remembered what Robert had told me about the rule that they had sworn to: monks may not possess anything of their own. Not even sleep. But don't bees each have their alveolus? I don't know anymore.

There was enough light to make out the contours of the room and the sleeping forms, but the world had lost its colour. At night, there are only black, white and countless shades of grey. I must have long known this, but I felt as though I were realizing it for the first time. How is it possible that eyes suddenly lose their ability to distinguish colours? Or is it the colours themselves that go away, returning at dawn? All I know is, there is no night darker than mourning.

Without lighting my lamp, I rose in silence and made my way, shivering, to the church of the abbey. The building site was deserted. Here and there I spotted piles of rocks like great beasts slumbering. The walls reached only halfway up, but even incomplete they were already vertiginous. It was as if Robert had sworn that his church would touch the heavens. Isn't that why it crumbled the first time? I advanced cautiously between the pillars and blocks of stone. The pre-dawn sky was milky pale. White dust swirled, flakes as numerous as the stars some evenings, disappearing as it touched the ground. I held out my palm: a tiny bite of cold. It was snowing inside the church.

The first sanctuary dedicated to Saint Michel was built in 708 in the rock at Mont Tombe, like the one at Monte Gargano, which inspired it. Before that, there was nothing, just a hole in the skull of a bishop charged with building it.

Notre-Dame-Sous-Terre was built on the orders of the holy man with the hole in his head, heeding the instructions of an archangel, which in turn were on the advice of a bull – the reason for which, no doubt, they would later call the bulk of the abbey La Merveille, the Wonder.

The story goes as follows: Aubert, the wise and pious bishop of Avranches, was visited in a dream by the archangel Michael, who commanded him to build a sanctuary. Forgetful or distracted, and in any event not in enough of a rush, the holy man failed to obey immediately. The angel was indulgent and visited him a second time, then a third. The third time, to be sure he was heard, he rested his finger of fire on the temple of the sleeping man, burning a hole into the bone that can still be admired today, because Aubert's skull and its hole rest in the Saint-Gervais d'Avranches Basilica.

So the bishop sent a few clerics to Monte Gargano in Italy, and they returned with a piece of Michael's scarlet coat, as well as a piece of the altar where he appeared and where the print of his heavenly foot can still be seen. The effect of these precious relics was soon felt. A blind woman from the hamlet of Astériac, not far from Mont Saint-Michel, suddenly recovered her sight. It was said that she cried, 'It is so beautiful to see!' The hamlet changed its name and still bears the name of Beauvoir – *beautiful to see.*

So Aubert chose to erect the sanctuary on the little island of Mont Tombe, deserted since the two hermits had left a century before. A bull was brought in, a crude but powerful animal, and tied to a picket, and it was decreed that the abbey would be erected wherever the beast trod the grass with its ancient hoof. The bishop was still unsure of how big the sanctuary should be, but he received another sign: the dew during the night fell on the summit of the mountain, except for one place that remained dry. It was a circular shape and could accommodate around a hundred people. That is where Notre-Dame-Sous-Terre was finally built.

Then the bishop found a local man, a good man, who, with the help of his twelve sons, laid the foundation for the sanctuary. It was a wasted effort: they couldn't finish the job. They had to bring a newborn baby to split the rock with his immaculate foot for construction to begin – yet more proof, if any more was needed, that sometimes there is no greater strength than weakness.

This is where legend ends and history begins. But the history of the construction (more fitting to say *constructions*) of the buildings of Mont Saint-Michel has plenty of holes, conjecture and supposition. You can consult records for the most-documented structures, study the plans executed in different eras, annotate everything, even scrutinize the models on exhibit at the site, but you will never have an accurate idea of the order in which the work was done or what Mont Saint-Michel looked like at any point in time.

But some things seem almost certain: the construction of the church at the abbey began around 1017 and lasted some sixty years. Since the rock was too hard to cut into or to level, they built around it, and the mountain showed through in many spots. This no doubt explains in part how trying to get one's bearings in the maze, real or on paper, that is Mont Saint-Michel, can make a person's head swim: the fact that the abbey is built not on the summit of a mountain, but around it. (Where its heart should be, it is empty, or rather full of rock.) The fact remains that the interior in no way resembles what the exterior suggests, and that the plans do not offer much in the way of understanding either. In a way, the abbey is indescribable.

Today, no matter what models or representations you study, it is virtually impossible to find your way through the series of rooms, which are more or less square and superimposed; it is like playing a game of snakes and ladders, taking two steps forward and four steps back, or looking at one of those drawings by Escher in which, at the end of a series of stairs that seem to go up, you have inexplicably come back down to the starting point. This may be due to the fact that construction was spread over half a millennium – a decidedly piecemeal approach – under the direction of different builders, each of whom had different skills and means from those of his predecessor – Gothic resting upon Romanesque set on Carolingian anchored in rock. Not to mention the collapses and fires over the years, and that a room built in 1100 could be partially destroyed one hundred years later, restored, modified again fifty years later and then two centuries after that.

Since the buildings couldn't sprawl across a large area, over the years construction continued upward. In the mid-twelfth century, the Abbot Robert de Torigni started work that changed the face of Mont Saint-Michel: he had two dungeons added, and a new, fairly modest residence that was meant for him, as well as a new, larger hostelry to receive the pilgrims who were flocking to the sanctuary. He also ordered two towers to be built flanking the church. The first housed a large number of the four hundred volumes that made up the library at the abbey, called at the time the City of Books. A considerable number of these works were lost when the tower collapsed about a decade after it was erected. The second fell in 1776.

In 1228, the construction of a three-storey double building was completed, with three dining rooms set one on top of the other (chaplaincy, guest house, refectory), intended for poor pilgrims, rich guests and monks, respectively. The rooms to the west were similarly organized: at the bottom, the cellar, meant for the needs of the body; in the middle, the scriptorium, dedicated to the work of the mind; and at the top, the cloister, a place of prayer and garden of the soul.

In the fifteenth century, the abbots were busy fortifying Mont Saint-Michel to defend it against the assault of the English, who had taken the entire province, including Tombelaine, the neighbouring island. Mont Saint-Michel was protected by a garrison of some two hundred men at arms sent by Charles VI. Cut off from revenue from sister abbeys across the channel, Mont Saint-Michel soon ran out of resources; that was no problem, however, as they melted the chalices and monstrances to mint the coins to pay the soldiers.

In 1421 or 1423, the choir of the church collapsed. It would take a century to rebuild it in pure flamboyant Gothic style. The room with the large pillars was erected first, ten columns like enormous roots that held the whole thing up, towering above, resting on a forest of exterior flying buttresses. For each shaft of light, a stone arch: two constructions, one mirroring the other.

In essence, Mont Saint-Michel does not house one abbey but rather ten, or even more, some of them now gone, phantom abbeys the building continues to bear the mark of, and other constructions modified over the centuries – all of it strung together and joined haphazardly. Gutted walls, collapsed vaults, ceilings burned, towers levelled, passages filled, stairs condemned, clock towers felled, rebuilt, crumbled in ruins; like a manuscript scribbled over ten times that bears the remnants of stories, traces of scratching and illegible characters, Mont Saint-Michel is an immense palimpsest set in rock.

The abbey has four gardens: the hortulus, the vegetable garden, where produce for everyday use is grown; the herbularius, where simples and medicinal plants are grown; the rose garden – and the library.

This morning, in the vegetable garden, I ran into Brother Clément, a pale, thin man with blue eyes so washed out they look almost white. He was busy cutting herbs that he then laid tidily in small bouquets in a wicker basket. A cat was following a few steps behind him.

He nodded at me without interrupting his work, and I studied the garden. This vegetable garden in the middle of the sky, in the middle of the sea, reminded me of the tale Anna told me about ancient Babylon, a city of hanging gardens where golden fruit grew and flowers bloomed only during the full moon.

They say that Brother Clément is a bit simple-minded. What he likes best from God is Creation, and from Creation, the humblest of plants. His prayers bear the names of *house-leek*, *St. John's wort*, *green bean*. He may sing off-key, but he plants straight as an arrow. The wooden crates in the vegetable garden were lined up in neat rows, each one holding two or three species of plants that are good bedfellows. He seems able to recognize plants by touch, if not solely by taste or smell. Robert says that he knows instinctively where to sow the seeds he receives from monks who bring them back from their travels or pilgrims who present them to him as an offering, and he guesses straightaway which shoot needs plenty of water and which one needs full sunlight. Services seem to be a gentle form of torture; he strains his face toward the door while the holy words are echoing, lightly scratching at the earth under his nails. Once the *Ite, missa est* is said, he is the first on his feet, rushing to reunite with his pods and his hulls.

Leaning my elbows on the ramparts, I watched the monks down below. Living among this old stone, they end up resembling it: most of them have dry hands, grey skin, cold eyes. For centuries the abbey was home to one of the most important libraries on the continent and a scriptorium where the monks came to translate Greek and Arabic, but today it is a shadow of its former self. It was Robert who made this sad observation. Knowledge has been lost, the love of work, the love of books – perhaps in reverse: first people stopped loving books, then the work no longer really interested anyone, and then knowledge disappeared. Scribes started making books quickly, with crude strokes, performing the task joylessly. Books were no longer a treasure.

Seen from above, the monks all looked alike with their brown cowls, the pale halos of the tonsures on the tops of their heads. They were small and interchangeable. Is this the way God sees man? God, or a bird? I managed to recognize each monk by his shadow, the movements of which I could follow, whereas the movements of the men escaped me, a curious reversal. The shadow bound to each one like a dog to its master suddenly appeared to me as a sort of dire premonition. Death was there, lying at our feet under the noonday sun, waiting patiently until we too would find ourselves stretched out on, and then under, the ground.

Men make war, they go on pilgrimages, they work the land and build cathedrals, every one of their gestures repeated by a silent twin. All that time, the monks, soldiers, princes and lepers don't realize that they are dancing with their own demise.

§

I asked to see the ossuary, and Brother Maximilien took me there. After going down several flights of stairs, the last of which was sculpted right into the rock, we pushed a heavy, wooden swinging door that closed behind us like the door of a tomb. Plunged in darkness, the room smelled of damp, moss and fungus. The only light was from our candles, which a mysterious draft caused to flicker, a circle of yellow light illuminating fingers and faces, gradually growing darker – gold, copper, bronze – as it advanced toward the walls, becoming black as soot.

Dozens of carefully piled skulls rested on the stone shelves, like turnips wintering in the cellar. Humeri, tibiae and femurs were placed below in bundles. Looking at them, I had the feeling, strange yet familiar, of looking into the eyes of a cat. But you cannot keep company with the dead without paying the price once you are back among the living. I can no longer look at an old man without seeing the bones under his skin, the hollow of his eyes and the hole for the nose.

The holy relics were kept elsewhere. There was nothing special about these bones. They all belonged to monks, since villagers are buried down below, in the tiny cemetery. Examining the skulls more closely, I did, however, notice that some were distinctly smaller. Child monks slept the same sleep as the others.

§

When I arrived, I spent the first days lying down, getting up only twice a day to eat and relieve myself, both with the same indifference. After a week, Robert came to see me. It must have been late in the morning. Sext had not yet been rung.

He told me, in his firm but quiet way, 'I would like you to attend services.'

'Why?'

What I wanted to say was, *To what end?*

'Because it is good to have the days governed by the rhythm of the holy hours, even for those who have not made a vow to devote themselves to God.'

I didn't answer, so he continued, his voice slightly mocking. 'And because I'm afraid that soon we will no longer be able to get you up in the morning, and I have no desire to carry you like a child.'

The monks celebrate God seven times a day – once in the middle of the night. Robert insisted that I attend at least two of the services, which I have been doing ever since.

In recent months, masses have been celebrated in the old underground church. When the choir of the abbey collapsed some thirty years ago, the monks simply erected a wall in the arch between the transept and the choir so they could keep celebrating mass there. It took months to clear the debris, assess the damage, shore up the structure to avoid more collapses; years to draw up the plans, raise the money needed for the work, choose the builder. During that time, the choir was covered with wooden slats to form a temporary roof, but it remained open to the elements. Still today, it is not unusual for it to rain in the choir. Birds have nested in there, and other vermin too, no doubt, among the beams and the struts. Underneath the choir a room was built with large pillars to support the structure that will climb higher and be more majestic than ever, if Robert is to be believed. The reconstruction work as such started shortly thereafter, and the monks moved their services underground until most of the structure was complete. Some twenty labourers are now working on the site morning to night, but their presence is hard to detect in the rest of the abbey. Most stay in the village, some for years. When I asked Robert when the new church would be ready, he answered, with his way of never seeming to take his own words seriously, 'Never.'

Between the stones of Notre-Dame-Sous-Terre, no more than fifteen monks remain today in the midst of the massive columns in the immense room meant to accommodate five times more. Their voices rise up, monotone and quaking within the walls. They seem to know that they too are about to disappear, to leave the rock to its solitude. But their singing still has a mournful beauty – or maybe it's me who can no longer hear anything beautiful without suffering.

In the middle of this morning's service, the grey cat crossed the nave with its light step. I jumped when I noticed it. Brother Maximilien, seated beside me, noticed my movement. He turned his head and, seeing the animal, crossed himself while making a face.

'Brother Clément's beast,' he whispered.

It was the first time he had spoken to me. I don't know why, among all of these silent monks, I had decided that this particular one was mute. I must have heard him singing, but that's when the voices come together to form just one, multiple yet indistinct. As if it had overheard his words, the cat turned its little head toward us and sat. The monk made a gesture to shoo it away, which the animal ignored.

'Where did he come from?' I asked.

Brother Maximilien shrugged before answering, in a disdainful whisper. 'I don't know. Probably from chasing vermin.'

I smiled and went on. 'Not the cat – Brother Clément. Where is he from?'

Brother Maximilien sniffed. 'No one knows. He showed up one morning with that filthy beast. He asked to be a lay brother, and he spent almost a year cleaning out the stables and feeding the chickens, without saying a word... Then by chance we discovered that he knew how to read and write, and he spoke Latin as fluently as if he had learned it at his mother's knee. To my way of thinking, no good comes of that sort of mystery. Why would a man of letters want to spend his days grooming horses – or growing lettuce?'

He stopped talking to be certain I agreed with him and to check that no one was looking our way disapprovingly, then he went on, still in hushed tones.

'In the end, since the abbey has more servants than it knows what to do with and very few literate monks, he was promoted without being asked his opinion. Besides, he doesn't seem to have one on most matters, and it must be said that since the garden was entrusted to him, the everyday food has improved tremendously.'

It seemed that the concession had cost Brother Maximilien a great deal. He tried to shoo the cat again, with a hiss that made four heads turn. He lowered his eyes as the animal calmly rose, throwing the shadow of a tiger on the wall.

§

Some monks, particularly the younger ones, are as thin as reeds, but there are a few who are as round as barrels. How this is possible, given their Spartan diet, remains a mystery.

At noon, we have a crust of bread to dip in a goblet of wine, an apple, a piece of cheese or a handful of beans. For the evening meal, we have stew made of beans and vegetables, wine that is often watered down and the rest of the bread. But some monks are as fat and soft as women who gorge themselves on candied fruit. Perhaps the answer lies not in the meals they joylessly eat, but in the hagiographies they ingest with their food: a spoonful of lentils, a good deed; a swig of wine, a psalm. Their bellies are swollen with edifying words, stories of saintly victims of torture offered as sustenance at mealtime.

The recitation of pious deeds blends with sounds of chewing and half-suppressed burps. No doubt what was intended, in imposing these readings, was to nourish the soul at the same time as the body, but I can't help but think that what was also intended was to remind the monks that they are mere mortals; they are not saints whose praise is sung, but men of flesh, humble eaters of beans and producers of wind.

I hadn't thought to inquire during our journey about what position Robert held at Mont Saint-Michel, and I barely gave it a thought in the first few weeks, which were spent in a fog that was almost starting to lift. The few times I went to the refectory, he was sometimes eating at one of the long tables where most of the brothers sat and sometimes he was in the company of a few others at a smaller table set on a slightly elevated platform. The monks definitely showed him respect and deference, but I thought it was mostly due to his erudition and natural authority. He had always been that way; even when we were children, he seemed older than the rest of us.

Just yesterday, I thought to ask him, albeit awkwardly, 'Are you in charge of the abbey?'

'God is the one in charge.'

Robert had been making this sort of observation since childhood. It was his way of answering a question by not answering or, rather, of not answering by answering. It had ceased to bother me a long time ago. I had learned to respond with a more specific question, one that he could not wriggle out of.

So I asked in another way. 'Are you in charge of it?'

'The responsibility is shared among the monks; each one has a role and a task.'

I had long believed that he did that not exactly to catch me out, but because he thought my questions pointless. I eventually understood that he wasn't this way just with me, and that he did it because he was careful never to make assumptions about the intentions of the person he was talking to. It could be irritating, often tedious, but it forced me to look at things in a new way, and sometimes even to consider ideas different from the ones I had begun to express at the start.

'Are you the abbot?' I asked. Usually I managed to get the answer I was after in three tries.

'No. His name is Guillaume d'Estouteville, and he lives in Rome. I'm just responsible for the day-to-day management of the abbey.'

This was said without emphasis, as if simply making an observation.

Since Robert was not fussy about food, he had more elaborate cooking done only when there were distinguished guests, or the vicars or procurators of the abbot himself, who had never visited the sanctuary he was responsible for. The rest of the time he settled for the same stew as the others, and a little less wine. Sometimes I would dine at his table when there were no important visitors; sometimes I would dine with silent monks.

The refectory had a diffuse light that seemed to emanate from the walls. No matter the vantage point, only one or two of the high, narrow windows were visible; they were set deep into the walls, letting the day filter in at equal intervals. The monks were all different under the tonsure and cowl, but since they never took either of them off, here too they appeared all alike, like variations of a single individual: a collection of sketches showing the same man, but from different angles, in different lights, at different stages of aging.

I made the remark to Robert, who answered, 'Their eyes are turned toward heaven, and their feet are in the dust. Their stomach is right between the two.'

And he lifted his eyes to the heavens, as if asking forgiveness or seeking witness.

I like to think that, over the centuries, successive churches have been built on Mont Saint-Michel by men from the same lineage. From father to son, they were the builders of the cathedral – the same one, never finished, which never stops growing, burning, climbing even higher, defiant, monumental, fragile.

The first of the family was a shepherd before becoming a stonecutter. He knew the bay like no one else, having walked along it in all kinds of weather with his bleating herd around him. He knew all the hazards, the sludge that could swallow a man and his steed, the tide that came in at a gallop, the fog that could sweep in like night falls. The bay had taught him prudence, but the sheep had taught him the art of watching where you step. He still missed them, their warm stench and their eyes so black they were blue. He thought of them when he was falling asleep and saw sparks spinning behind his eyelids.

Working suspended between heaven and earth, the second in line discovered that he liked men only from a distance. Once he came back down, their petty ugliness showed. But from his perch, he had the leisure of imagining them as he would have liked them to be. It was for those small, faceless men that he was building a church in the middle of the sky.

Then there were a few generations of unexceptional artisans, capable of copying what their predecessors had done, not taking anything away or adding anything new. Since dead things are less abrasive than living ones, in some cases the imitations were more pleasing to the eye than the original. And then there was an exceptionally talented worker, who died so young that all that remains as testimony to his genius is a single stone. If the entire abbey collapsed, his stone would remain. After his death, a son was born who had no taste for heights and no love for stone. He was a fisherman, and he too died in the prime of his life, without producing a son. His daughter, on the other hand, had learned as a child how to handle a chisel and hammer; she was responsible for some of the abbey's most delicate friezes and the profiles of certain angels.

She had a son who lived to be one hundred years old and who worked until his dying day. Hunched and grey, he continued to sculpt the rock long after losing his sight – fingers don't go blind. He showed to other men the same kindness normally reserved for young children: absent-minded, patient and weary. He left a legacy of small, perfectly round columns and forests of finely chiselled leaves.

His son learned from him by watching, but mostly by looking at the clouds. He built using rock because he didn't know how to sculpt blocks of sky. But in truth, he didn't build with rock; he built in the spaces between the rocks. Under the cross, with arms spread like the yard of a foremast, the rocks served only to frame the essential: the light, which unfurled in golden waves in the nave, at once church and ship.

§

The vagaries of history and the digressions of the French language are such that today we use the same word to say that we have faith and to name the instrument of torture that Christ died on: *je crois/une croix, I believe/a cross*.

And yet *croire*, French for *to believe*, comes from the same root as *coeur*, or *heart* (*credo*, from the Indo-European *kred*, is related to *cor, cordis*), whereas *croix*, French for *cross*, comes from the *circus* family, or *curve* (*crux: circus, curvus*). The cross is a gallows, but also, potentially, something that spins

– some maintain that the swastika, a twisted, perverted cross, is inspired by a representation of the sun in motion. *Crois* and *croix* (a heart/a solar circle; a centre/a periphery; an inside/an outside) seem virtual opposites, but they have the same consonants rolling in the mouth, the same vowels uttered. Today, by metonymy, the Christian faith, of which the cross is a symbol, just as the Creed is the purest expression of it, is often designated in French by the simple word *croix*. Both *crois* and *croix*, *believe* and *cross*, have been superimposed and fused to form just one.

I think the Creed is the only prayer that we had to learn by heart at Collège Jésus-Marie, where we also had to attend a mass celebrated at the school chapel a few times a year. Those who wanted to would rise to take communion; I would stay seated. The priest, always the same one, was a stout, pot-bellied man in his forties. When he spoke, thick saliva formed at the corners of his mouth, giving the words of the gospel a pasty feel. The chapel itself was a brand-new room, furnished in blond wood and devoid of mystery. The old college had burned to the ground a few years earlier, and the old stones, the creaking floors, the high, nineteenth-century windows, had been replaced by a concrete building that looked like a comprehensive school.

The Creed was one of the few things – perhaps the only thing – that we recited in a chorus, in monotone, a hundred voices united. My parents had recited it too, some forty years earlier (at the time, they also had to make novenas, attend mass every morning in the month of May and whatever else), as did their parents before them (at that time, the rosary was said as a family, around the radio set). In the white chapel that still smelled of fresh wood, I was completely cut off from that; this prayer had belonged to them, and they abandoned it, but it was never mine.

§

For the Romans, the word *fides* meant something different from what today we call *faith* – in French, *foi* – and had nothing to do with belief. The concept was similar to what we now associate with *good faith*; it had to do with honesty, integrity, a person's reliable character, particularly when party to an agreement or contract. The notion was so important that Fides was made a goddess by Numa Pompilius. This *fides* that gave us *faith* didn't mean the fact of believing but the virtue we believed in: the object rather than the action. I realize in writing this that I am not unlike the old Romans: I have never had faith in God, but I believe strongly in faith.

It is surely not by chance that we now use the same word for a person who embraces religion and a person who, in a marriage or union, remains constant and does not look for love elsewhere: *faithful*. In both cases, faith and trust are represented in equal part.

Before houses of stone or wood, we live in cabins of words, trembling, with rays of light peeking through. We say *I love you* to feel warm; we say *orange* and we sniff our fingers; we say *it's raining* for the pleasure of staying inside, curled up next to the light of the word *book*. (The French word for *book* is *livre*, which comes from *liber*: the living part of tree bark, but also *liberté*, *liberty*.)

Of course the world is there, and things exist, but we can always change them or make them disappear by snapping our fingers, by saying *I don't love you anymore*. Or *I believe*.

When he found me, Robert said that he had heard about what had happened to me thanks to divine Providence. I didn't tell him that I would call that chance. As so often happened, we were talking about the same thing and something completely different, as if we were living in two separate worlds that connect only in appearance. In any case, he was in Paris to meet a cleric from the university and look for a handful of books, some of which were to be returned to the Mont Saint-Michel library and some he hoped to have copied.

There was nothing terribly rare or precious among them; for close to two centuries, the abbey's library and scriptorium had been virtually abandoned. Only a handful of monks toiled away there, one of them with a trembling hand and another with pupils so clouded that sometimes he mistook one word for another and, rather than recopying the wisdom of the ancients, he invented inanities that he committed to paper for centuries to come. People would still come from a far-off university or monastery to consult the books at Mont Saint-Michel, remarkable for their rarity or the excellence of their execution, but invariably the books had been created over a century before. This he told me in snippets, evening by evening, when we were done walking and were sitting in front of the fire. Maybe he wanted me to know what to expect when we arrived; maybe he simply needed to tell himself the story of his abbey again.

One day he admitted to me, 'Sometimes I have the impression that I'm the steward of a monument that people come to admire the ruins of, or the keeper of a menagerie with nothing more to show than a couple of hares, a dozen rats, a stuffed fox and a basilisk.'

I didn't know what to say.

He straightened his shoulders and went on, as if trying to convince me. 'And yet, the library is still alive. It is our shared memory, without which we are children feeling our way in the dark.'

I had absent-mindedly agreed. I was barely alive myself. All I wanted to do was sleep.

In the city, he had walked the streets asking after me. When asked to describe me, he said I had brown hair, was thin, with blue eyes, of average height. In truth, it had been so long since he had seen me that he no longer knew what I looked like. Yet, seeing a drunk staggering in a doorway, he recognized me right away, he said. I had recognized him too, but I thought I was dreaming, and I slapped my arms to try to chase the vision away. And then I put myself in his hands.

§

We started our journey the very same day, and we walked for almost a week, exchanging hardly a word.

One evening, we stopped at an inn on the side of the road. The common room was full, and Robert asked that food be brought to our room upstairs. I sat on the bed, amazed at how saggy it was. Robert, who had asked for a quill and ink, started scribbling out some correspondence. The tip of the quill on the parchment scratched like an insect. The light was fading in the room. Outside, the whinny of travellers' horses could be heard, along with the hoarse *cock-a-doodle-doo* of a rooster greeting the evening.

We were brought broth, bread, a roast chicken, an omelette and vegetable stew, all of which we ate in silence. At one point, Robert looked at me and said, 'The trick is to stay upright and keep walking.'

I listened to his words in a sort of stupor, sucking on a bone and then my greasy fingers. Through the window, in the fading day, I saw part of the yard, beyond the trees, at the end of the road that climbed the hill and disappeared in fields bathed in shadow. I tilted my head to the side, and a bubble in the uneven glass distorted the branches of the plane tree outside, thin and black like a spider's legs. The walls of the stables started to ripple up to the roof, which looked like it was about to collapse. The moon, low in the sky, looked like a threadbare piece of fabric. All this made me feel a little sick, or maybe it was because I had eaten too much. I closed my eyes, breathed in deeply, breathed out and opened my eyes again. In vain. The world was still there.

Most often, we slept in kennels or cowsheds, warmed by the animals. The peasants from whom we asked permission to spend the night offered us their beds, but Robert consistently refused, assuring them that Our Lord had chosen oxen and donkeys for warmth, so their company would be good enough for us, humble travellers that we were. The farmers never knew how to respond: in silence they went to get blankets, prepared two straw mattresses in the animals' beds and then left their own barn, speaking in hushed tones, as if they were leaving a church.

But sometimes night would fall when there was no village in sight, not even the most meagre of farms. Robert would leave the road to find a shallow ravine or a patch of clover. He would make a fire, spread his coat on the ground and roll up in it as best he could, while I sat there watching the flames late into the night. I would end up drifting off to sleep without realizing it, and I would wake up at dawn, shivering. Robert would still be sleeping, wrapped in his cowl, and the fire would be nothing but embers and black cinders.

§

One night, however, I woke with a start. Three men dressed in rags towered over me, their faces obscured by beards, their mouths a slash between their ears. If the three of them had pooled their teeth, they might have had enough for a smile. By the light of the fire, their oily skin had glints of orange.

The one closest to me held a small dagger. Reaching out, he said, 'Hand it over.'

I answered, 'I don't have any money,' adding without real conviction, 'We are poor pilgrims.'

One of his associates kicked Robert in the ribs, and he opened his eyes. He sat up and looked at me with an inscrutable expression. There was no fear, no surprise – something like disappointment, maybe, or resignation.

'That one's a monk!' said the man who woke me up, and he burst into a throaty laugh.

But the second one, the smaller one, pushed me aside in one gesture and moved in to get a closer look at Robert. 'Is it true, Brother, that you're a monk?' he asked, with a touch of reverence in his voice.

'It's true.'

'What difference does that make?' the first one said, growing impatient. 'Come on, hand it over,' he repeated, bringing the blade closer to my neck.

He had barely any teeth, and one of his eyes closed when he spoke. I remembered, in another life, having painted a demon with a similar physiognomy. A pointier nose, perhaps, a more cunning look. Instinctively, I lowered my eyes to look for hooves, but the man had rags wrapped around his feet. He looked ordinary, except for the poor coat of mail he wore over his rags and the axe he held in his hand.

'Maybe the Brother can forgive us our sins,' the little one said, and his two companions froze, astonished.

'Really?' asked the first, whose blade still hovered near my throat.

One by one they kneeled before Robert and rattled off a litany that would have been funny had it not been for the first man's dagger, the second man's axe and the third man's club.

> *I killed a man*
> *stole a chicken*
> *shared my sister's bed*
> *lied to my mother*
> *cursed*
> *cut flour with lime*
> *slept with a goat*
> *ate meat on Friday*
> *blinded a dog*
> *cut off a cat's tail*
> *poached on the seigneur's land*
> *set fire to the neighbour's barn*
> *tricked, betrayed my faith, stole, robbed, committed larceny,*
> *cheated, pilfered, plundered, harried, ransacked, mocked,*
> *marauded, pillaged*
> *Brother, forgive me.*

Robert made the sign of the cross over the three heads crawling with lice. Two of the men wanted to get up when the third one asked, 'Can you forgive us for all the rest, too?'

'The rest?'

'The sins we haven't committed yet?'

The other two locked eyes, frozen in admiration. I heard a short burst of laughter, and it took me a second to realize that it had come from me. The three bandits glowered at me. I coughed, careful not to move a muscle.

The smallest of the three continued, in an even voice, 'Like having killed a monk and his companion.'

Silence fell again. The night held its breath for a moment. Calmly, Robert absolved them. The three men got up, shook their heads as if they were emerging from the water. They hesitated a moment and then turned on their heels.

And then, I swear, when they were about ten steps away, Robert called them back.

'Hey!'

I grabbed his arm and squeezed it. He smiled gently.

'You forgot this.'

He threw them his leather purse with its jingling coins. The tall one, who was armed with a club, lunged for it, but the other two held him back. The one carrying the axe shook his fist and shouted something. They disappeared into the shadows. Knees trembling, I went to pick up the purse while Robert stoked the fire and then rolled up in his coat again.

The sounds of the night seemed to come back one by one: the leaves rustled in the breeze, invisible insects chirred, somewhere a tree creaked. Above our heads, the stars made a powdery streak in the sky.

There were no further mishaps during our trip. It took us three weeks and six days to reach Mont Saint-Michel. I later learned that Robert normally travelled by wagon or, at least, on horseback. I smiled, thinking I had forced him to make a sort of pilgrimage, and then I thought that maybe he was the one who had needed this long journey on foot.

§

We arrived at Mont Saint-Michel in fog. The entire bay was cloaked in a white cloud that lifted as we reached the abbey. It appeared suddenly, as if emerging from the water.

In spite of my exhaustion and the hunger that plagued me, it took my breath away. At that moment, I understood in a flash how I should have painted Anna's eyes: tear down this abbey and crush its rocks down to the last stone, one by one tear the silver scales from the backs of the fish, break open the oysters to scrape out their nacre, hollow out the eyes of birds that see the sky from on high, mix all that with sea water and the rain from clouds over the bay, wait for a ray of sun to come drink, kill it.

Robert slowed his step, and he too looked at the rock that turned into a church rising up to the sky.

I stopped next to him.

His mouth was half-open, his eyes shining. He must have looked that way twenty years earlier when he arrived at Mont Saint-Michel for the first time. He muttered to himself:

And God said: Let there be a firmament in the midst of the waters and let it divide the waters from the waters.

And God made the firmament, and divided the waters which were under the firmament from the waters which were above the firmament: and it was so.

And God called the firmament Heaven.

He had just witnessed the second day of Creation, once again.

He turned to me, but I was no longer looking at the massive construction of rock perched on buttresses; I was contemplating its shimmering reflection in the water of the bay. Dwarfed by such terrible grandeur, I had sought refuge in the abbey the sun drew on the sand. I preferred the image to the model, the shadow to the rock.

E very day my daughter and I walk through the deserted summer streets of Outremont. There is a dusty, golden light, still trees, the outline of Mont Royal nearby, but we don't hear its birds.

I still don't know whether we'll stay here or go live (for good? if not, for how long?) in Boston. I feel like we have already left but never arrived: I have a constant sense of floating that never leaves, even in my sleep. I am looking for a place where we can settle, where we can rest.

We stop for a moment to throw bread to the ducks. The ducklings are growing before our very eyes; they are already almost as plump as the mother. Soon the males will get their colours, and then, when the first cold hits, they will be off. I wonder whether the same ones come back every year, whether, like salmon, they remember where they were born. My daughter was born three blocks from here, on the fourth floor of Block 9 of the Saint-Justine Hospital, at the beginning of winter, one week before Christmas.

§

At the end of the summer, we are on the coast of Maine. The waves roll along the beach, sending pebbles and clamshells tumbling, gently knocking together like dice shaken in the palm of a hand.

The marshes reflect pools of sky, the same colour as the sea whispering in the distance. Floating in them are three ducks, two geese and one cloud. The sea breeze carries the smell of salt and kelp, the odour of the limestone from shells that have survived the ages. A heron, all leg and beak, stands still for a while in the marsh, water up to its knees, before diving in a flash and jabbing at its reflection. With great lumbering steps, it heads into the ocean's narrowing fingers, amid the reeds and puddles of cloud.

When night falls, all you can hear is the murmur of the waves and the metallic song of the frogs in the darkness. Nearby, invisible from the road or the beach, there is a cemetery you can access through a hole in the fence: a dozen wobbly tombstones, faded with the years, passengers on a ship that headed for Boston in July 1807 and sank not far off the coast. Among them, Lydia Carver, a young woman who was going to the big city to buy her trousseau in anticipation of her upcoming nuptials, and whose ghost still haunts the land her family owned.

My time used to be my own, shared with books. Now every moment devoted to reading or writing is a moment not spent with my daughter; writing has developed a dreadful urgency and a nagging guilt. It is time that I'm stealing from her, that I can't get back, that I should have devoted to her and that I will not have spent with her. Since her birth, I find myself thinking in the future anterior and the past conditional, complicated tenses that are signs of looking at things from a point of view other than the one we normally speak from: tomorrow seen as the past, yesterday as a possibility.

She is sleeping. I should take advantage of the time to write, but all I can do is sink into the sound of the waves. I would like to stretch out on the sand, stay there until night, let myself be swept out by the tide.

There were places in the immense abbey that are over-populated. Several days a month, the monks, who have taken a vow of silence and exiled themselves to a rock in the middle of the sea, are assailed by crowds; it's like being in the middle of the old slums of Paris. And just like in the city, among the pilgrims who flock to Mont Saint-Michel, there are bandits, outlaws, thieves and scoundrels of all sorts. While the almonry barely manages to accommodate the poor who have come to pray to the archangel, the guest hall is empty every other day: the rich don't have as much reason to pray, or they prefer to do it quietly at home. The hordes that arrive and retreat create a sort of second tide around the Mont, capricious, noisy and flea-infested. The bowels of the abbey are teeming with people, but the monks do their best to ignore the crowds that distract them from prayer and contemplation. Perhaps there is no greater silence than in the midst of clamour.

Since the abbot lives in Rome, his apartments here are almost always cold and vacant. Robert does not use them. But as of yesterday, the large rooms are housing one of his two vicars, his guests and aides, for a two-week stay. For the past three days, the kitchen has been busy roasting piglets and shaping almond paste, which it seems Vicar Thibaud is particularly fond of. This childlike taste surprised me, but in approaching him for the first time, I noticed that he gave off a faint whiff of vanilla. He is a handsome man, with somewhat weary features, dressed in a luxurious robe, and he was sitting by the fire waiting for us. The walls of the modestly sized room were decorated with fleurs-de-lys and colourful motifs reminiscent of the illuminations in some of the manuscripts that Robert had showed me, as if the abbey itself were an enormous book.

'Vicar,' Robert said once we'd entered, 'this is my cousin. I told you about him.'

The vicar raised his eyes from the mother-of-pearl case he was examining and seemed surprised to see us there. He raised his hand in a distracted, elegant gesture.

'Of course, your cousin.' He paused almost imperceptibly before adding with confidence, 'Antoine.'

'Éloi,' Robert gently corrected him.

'Éloi, yes.' Then, choosing to ignore my mud-streaked hose and long beard, but not without first shooting them a quick glance, 'They tell me you are a famous sculptor.'

Robert didn't give me time to answer. 'With all due respect, Éloi is a painter, Father.'

'A painter? What a shame. We have such a great need for someone to get to work on our poor friezes. But,' he continued, 'since you know how to handle a paintbrush, you can learn to use a hammer, can't you?'

I bowed wordlessly.

And then, no doubt thinking the civilities had gone on long enough, he began to inquire about Robert's trip. Robert gave him a succinct account, omitting most of our misadventures, particularly the night we were almost murdered.

'And what have you brought us?' the vicar finally asked.

His tone reminded me of the one used by the lord for whom Robert's father was steward when he asked what his cook had found at the market.

Robert unwrapped his package in silence and pulled out two leather-bound volumes. The first, small and black, was thin and looked worn. The vicar stroked the cover before picking it up. Discovering a series of calculations inside, he couldn't hide a pout.

'It is a famous treatise on algebra, Father,' Robert said.

'Of course,' the vicar answered, holding out his other hand.

Robert placed the second volume in his hand, a book as large as two palms, the cover of which was blank. Thibaud seemed curious and opened it to the middle, quietly read a few lines, repeated them louder, knitting his eyebrows.

> *'I have a marvellous hat,' said Aïmer, 'made from the skin of a marine fish, and it makes a man invisible...'*

He raised his eyes to Robert, who was smiling at the words. I was smiling too, imagining the fish-skin hat on the head of the most serious vicar. I was hoping he would continue reading.

'Perhaps you have heard about this gest,' Robert said. 'It is not as famous as *The Song of Roland*, but it belongs to the same family. It's called *The Pilgrimage of Charlemagne*.'

'*The Song of Roland* was the tale of the heroic true Battle of Roncevaux,' the vicar said, interrupting him. 'Do you mean to say that our esteemed emperor on a pilgrimage to the Holy Land had nothing better to do than to listen to such drivel? A fish-skin hat that makes you invisible!'

'No, of course not. The song is not supposed to tell the truth: it tells a tale; it is a fantasy.'

'And it is that fantasy that you have brought back to stand alongside the Holy Scriptures in our library?'

'With the treatise on mathematics, Father.'

The vicar was still holding the two books in his open hands, as if he were the scale responsible for determining their relative weight. Suddenly he laid both down before him.

'Very well then, good evening,' he said to dismiss us, and we left bowing.

When we left the room, I said, 'You didn't show him everything.'

Robert raised his eyebrows, spread his arms and opened his hands as if to show that they were empty. A smile played on his lips. 'Has it ever happened that you found a drawing so extraordinary that you couldn't share it with anyone?' he asked.

'A drawing, no.'

But the model.

'Some things are made to be exhibited, shared with as many as possible. There are books that are lanterns or beacons, and their light guides men through the shadows of this world.'

'And that one?'

'That one is not a light; it is a fire that could set entire kingdoms ablaze.'

I remembered the work: it was a small worn book with rounded corners, probably bound in calfskin, that gave off a slightly mildewed odour. I hadn't seen it again since we arrived at the abbey. I looked at Robert, but he was no longer looking at me. He was still smiling to himself, as if the fire of this mysterious book were burning somewhere behind his eyes.

In the cloister, the monks were walking in silence. When I looked inside, I saw a carefully planned garden, the tender green of lettuce. Outside, the bay stretched into the distance, then the sea, then the sky. That day, like other days, I had the impression of being both inside and outside, as if in a space that did not quite belong to the abbey but that was already somewhat in the clouds. I always felt a little dizzy walking around it.

'What is in the book?' I asked Robert, who was walking beside me.

He looked to see that no one was around before stopping. He pulled the book from his cowl, opened it and slowly turned the pages. I wanted to remind him that the characters made no sense to me, but soon he stopped at an image with spheres of different sizes.

'The same thing as in a lot of others, you see,' Robert said. 'The Sun, the Earth, the Moon, the planets and the stars.'

Squinting, I studied the drawing. While precise, it had been carelessly executed, by a confident but hurried hand.

The large yellow orb was the Sun, that much was obvious. It was in the middle. The smaller ones seemed to be set around it in no particular order. Among them, indifferently and off-centre: the Earth. I raised my eyes to Robert's.

'That can't be right,' I said.

He smiled at me. 'And with that you are saying what many have said, and important people at that: people like Aristotle; like Ptolemy, who in the *Great Treatise* showed the position of the Earth at the centre of the heavens; like Theon of Alexandria ... '

He started walking again. Spandrels scrolled by before our eyes. I noticed distractedly that each one had different foliage – the cloister is a forest where no two trees are alike.

'I don't know the ins and outs of this,' I replied awkwardly, 'but I know that I'm not moving, nor is this abbey, and that the spoon I set on the table will not fly off as it would if the Earth was truly rotating around the Sun.'

'And you have said nothing about what our good and wise vicar would say if by some misfortune he noticed this book – that is, that the Bible establishes that the Sun has revolved around the Earth since the beginning of time.'

I was relieved to see that he too saw that the drawing was impossible and incorrect.

'But then what good is the book if it is filled with lies?' I asked.

'First of all, we don't know that they are lies. We know that we do not understand how it could be true, which says a great deal about us, little about the book and even less about the world. It was written over one thousand five hundred years ago by a scholar named Aristarchus of Samos. There are probably only two or three copies left in the world. A handful of men have read it; some of them may have thrown it in the fire afterward. Others no doubt burned it instead of reading it. But it is not for us to burn books; we are here to protect them, just as we would save the last creatures threatened by the rising waters, even the dangerous ones.'

I was not convinced. Of course I recognized the allusion to Noah, but I told myself that we may not have lost a great deal had we decided not to take the snakes and spiders on board.

'Why the dangerous ones too?' I asked.

'Who are you to decide?' he answered. Then, as if admitting that that was not a real answer, he added, 'Because to be able to read the good ones, sometimes you have to have read the ones that are considered bad. Books talk to each other before they talk to us.'

Robert kept walking, while I stood there, pensive. It was then that I understood where my vertigo came from. It was not because I was walking in the middle of the sky above the water; it was the series of small columns set regularly in staggered rows, which seemed to advance while I remained where I was.

Cloister, from the Latin *claustrum*, meaning *enceint, enclosure*.

In French, the words *femme enceinte*, for *pregnant woman*, have always seemed strange to me. When I was little, for a long time I heard *femme en ceinte*, or *a woman in something or other*... as if describing a woman who was in love, in need or in a pair of pants – basically a fleeting state that was, grammatically speaking, a matter of qualification rather than determination. Things didn't improve when I looked into what the word meant. According to the authoritative *Trésor de la langue française*, the verb *enceindre* meant *to surround, contain within certain limits*. And yet, it would seem that a pregnant woman is not surrounded, nor contained. In fact, it is just opposite: she is the one doing the containing.

I ended up solving the puzzle the day I understood that the word *enceinte* should not be heard as an adjective, but as a noun. A pregnant woman is not a woman who is enclosed by something, but a woman who forms the enclosure. A woman cloister.

When we went for the first ultrasounds, as they handed over the silky paper that showed my daughter's profile – bulging forehead, button nose, ghostly fingers – we were told to take pictures of them. It seems that after a few years, the images on the paper dissolve. It's something to do with the ink, I think. So we took pictures of the pictures.

Now we have a digital copy stored on computer, which doesn't seem more durable than the poorly set powder on slippery paper. Either way, there is something fleeting about it.

Everyone knows that we continue to see the light of distant stars long after they are dead. But we never think about stars just born. If we can still see the sparkle of dead stars, there are suns whose light we don't yet see, and yet they are there, blazing in the darkness, completely imperceptible.

Once they have taken in the holy relics, most visitors of any importance ask, if only to be polite, to see the library. Robert or Brother Louis show them the same twelve books, all produced three or four centuries ago. The reds on the parchment have turned the brown of dried blood, the blues have faded, the greens have turned grey, but they are praised all the same. Some also try to pay a visit to Aubert's skull, a favour that is granted parsimoniously to a few guests. So far no one has asked to see the garden, or the gardener.

'People from all over talk about it. I am curious to explore it,' Brother Adelphe said at breakfast. He arrived with Vicar Thibaud, whom he advises on I don't know what, and who has to leave in a few days.

The vicar and Brother Louis seemed equally astonished. In an abbey like this, who would want to smell flowers rather than study texts?

'If you will permit me, I would like to have a few minutes of the time of the person responsible for the herbularius and the vegetable garden,' Adelphe said.

'The vegetable and medicinal gardens are both Brother Clément's responsibility, if I'm not mistaken,' Thibaud replied tentatively, seeming to dread that Adelphe, wanting to make conversation, would find himself face to face with an odd fellow caked in dirt who was shaking carrot plants.

Robert confirmed by nodding his head.

'I will take you there after breakfast, if you like,' the vicar offered.

'Don't go to any trouble. I can find it on my own.'

And indeed, after the meal, he went down the garden path unescorted.

I would be lying if I said that I overheard their conversation by chance. In truth, I wanted find out what Brother Adelphe was curious about, and I also wanted to again see Brother Clément, who until this point I had seen only as he hurried by. I spent a few minutes wandering the pathways, breathing in the flowers and herbs. The gardens are indeed remarkable, not for their size, which is modest, of course, given the limited space the gardener has between the buildings and the rock, but for the intelligence of their design. The plants grow in a perfectly ordered fashion, like a miniature city, and yet walking among them is like walking through a small forest that has shot up completely naturally. How this is possible I do not know; it would seem that vegetables also have their mysteries. While musing on this, I settled into a corner, behind a fragrant grove, and that was when I saw the visitor coming. From my position, I could quietly observe without being seen.

Kneeling in front of a planter with green tops rising out of it, Brother Clément was unearthing pale, tapered roots, a bit longer than a hand, the tips of which were spiked with hairs. A few similar roots, only finer, were already in the basket at his side. He started when Brother Adelphe greeted him. The grey cat sitting near him jumped up and bolted.

'Is that parsley you have there?' Brother Adelphe asked, in the polite tone of a man who has found a pretext for conversation.

Placing his hand on the basket, Clément answered, 'Parsnips, Brother. Very common. We use them in soups and purées. The monks like them because they are sweet.'

The visitor looked at the stems Brother Clément held in his hand, then at his face, which was looking at him, unblinking.

'A humble vegetable,' the visitor finally opined, 'which will see a family of peasants through the harshest of winters.'

Clément nodded his head and carefully placed the plants upside down in his basket so that the leaves lined up with the roots of those that were already in it.

'I have heard that you have one of the most bountiful gardens in the duchy,' Adelphe continued.

'I cannot take the credit.'

'Not at all: I see species here that I have only ever seen in books. There, isn't that cardamom? How did you get it?'

As he said this, he picked a small green pod and rubbed the husk between his fingers. A fragrance spread through the branches that I had never smelled before: sweet, wild and heady.

'The abbey receives pilgrims from all over,' Brother Clément explained. 'Some bring gifts of books or relics, others seeds or cuttings. Some have even received them from other travellers. Dozens of seeds were waiting to be planted when I was entrusted with the gardens. Some I was able to identify only once the plant reached maturity, thanks to its flower or fruit. There are others that, even after they have budded, remain a mystery. But it is good to try to make the humblest of plants bloom, along with knowledge...'

Brother Adelphe listened in silence. I thought that it was a wise reflection for a mere gardener who was supposedly simple-minded as well. As if he had had the same thought, Brother Clément added, 'At least, that is what our librarian says, a learned and wise man.'

'And in fact it requires tremendous wisdom to know not only how to read, but also how to write in the great book of nature,' Brother Adelphe said. 'Shall we walk a little?'

Without waiting, Brother Adelphe took a few steps, continuing his train of thought. 'And, like books, sometimes nature lies to us or tries to fool us. For example, do you have a plant called the mandrake here?'

'I have never seen it.'

'But you know of it, don't you?'

Brother Clément was silent for a moment, as if wondering what he was supposed to answer. I was afraid they would walk away from me, which would have prevented me from following the rest of their conversation, but Adelphe stopped almost immediately to look at a shrub with small flowers.

'I have heard stories about it that cannot be repeated here, in a place of meditation and prayer.'

This did not discourage Brother Adelphe, who continued, 'That it grows under the feet of the hanged and soaks up their seed; that it even has two arms and two legs, that it is a plant made into a man.'

'Or man made into a plant,' said Brother Clément. 'Which is an even greater aberration.'

They continued their walk in silence, Brother Adelphe stopping from time to time to rustle a bush and breathe in the fragrance or to pluck a leaf that he would chew pensively. The cat, which had come out of hiding, was following at a distance, stopping when they stopped, as if it too were eavesdropping on their conversation.

For a few minutes, I could no longer see them. A bee was buzzing around me, and I tried to shoo it off without too much noise or movement, afraid of giving away my presence if they came back. After a few minutes, they headed down a nearby pathway without noticing me. I craned my head while keeping an eye on the bee that had landed on the tip of my toe.

'These are parsnips,' Brother Adelphe said quietly, pointing to the shoot of plants in Brother Clément's wicker basket.

Then, pointing again without brushing the two roots set head to tail, 'But not those.'

'No,' Clément confirmed.

'Do you know what they are?'

'Yes.'

'And it was you who grew them?'

'Yes.'

'There's no chance that someone could pick them accidently?'

'No. I'm the only one who has access to this part of the herbularius, and I'm the only one who picks the plants here.'

The visitor studied him carefully and then said, 'I'm not telling you anything you don't already know when I say that hemlock is one of the most dangerous plants in existence. It was used to put Socrates to death.'

I shuddered. I didn't know this Socrates, but I had heard about hemlock.

'But it is also used to treat certain malignant tumours,' Clément answered.

'Of course, as a poultice, in women whose breast is infected. Are you hiding a woman here somewhere, Brother Clément?'

Clément smiled a bit sadly. 'It is not just used for women.'

'Are you sick? Or one of the brothers?'

Clément didn't answer but looked down at the ground. I did the same. In the earth a beetle was running fitfully, protected by his pathetic shell. The insect and his armour were no bigger than a thumb.

The day of my second visit to Mont Saint-Michel, almost five years ago, after visiting the rooms open to tourists, we looked in vain for the way leading to the lace staircase, only to find out that it was now off limits to visitors. I remembered having climbed it as a teenager, among the forest of flying buttresses, and having looked out over the roofs and the bay down below, dizzy not from the altitude but from seeing the world from a completely different angle for the first time.

That day, we instead stopped in the rose garden right beside the quiet cemetery where the villagers are buried. He kneeled on the ground and pulled a beautiful old ring out of his bag, which he slid on my finger. It should have been the most memorable moment of the day (of the trip, of the year), but I remember more clearly the breakfast we had eaten a few hours before, in the bedroom of the old stone house overlooking the sea, in Cancale. The villa was deserted, the tray had been laid silently in front of our door. There were croissants and butter with a Norman stamp, marmalade, fresh-squeezed orange juice, a thin crêpe, yogurt in a small glass jar, tea for me, fragrant with bergamot, and for him, café au lait. We could see the turquoise sea through the open window, like in the tropics, and in the distance, pale on the horizon, the silhouette of Mont Saint-Michel stood in the middle of the water.

§

This abbey does not represent today what it did one thousand years ago, obviously. But what did people feel within these walls in 1015 or 1515? What did people feel outside these walls? For a long time, I worried about not being able to write a book set at a time when the potato was still unknown. This was not a metaphor; I didn't want to say *a world in which America didn't exist as such yet*, but truly a world where no one had ever tasted a potato.

They lived on a planet at the centre of the firmament, around which the sun and moon rotated, a world created in seven days and organized by divine will. The planet had just one enormous continent. The plague hit every few decades, leprosy and war raged the rest of the time. Few people had seen a book, even fewer knew how to make heads or tails of it. Witches slept with the devil and poisoned well water. People healed themselves with lead powder, which a few sorcerers knew how to turn to gold.

The most difficult thing, in trying to write about the past, is not trying to find the lost science, faith or legends, or making gargoyles and stone carvers reappear; it is forgetting the world as we know it. It means, in the present day, erasing everything that was not yet, everything that existed but escaped being seen or heard. How do you do without half of what we know and not suddenly feel half-deaf and half-blind? How do you forget the smell of tobacco, the taste of chocolate and the red of tomatoes? How can you not help but see a potato-shaped hole on every table?

§

When I was little, Radio-Canada broadcast a soap opera called *Le parc des braves*, set between the wars. I remember watching it, bored, but also with a sort of distracted curiosity, like finding a picture with the face not of someone I knew but of someone who is related to that person. The hairstyles, the clothing, the physiognomy even, were familiar: it was set almost in the time of my father's childhood, which he often talked to me about.

One day, when we were watching the show, he asked me: 'Do you think people who lived between the wars knew they were living between two wars?'

I thought about it. I had never considered. I ventured, 'No...'

'Why not?'

'Um... Obviously there were people who died before the second... Or who were born after the first...'

I was avoiding the question: those people were indeed living between two wars, but had only lived through one of the two. I wasn't satisfied with my answer, but I couldn't come up with a better one.

'And?' my father asked, prodding me.

I was silent.

'They knew there had been one war,' he went on, 'but they couldn't have known there would be another one, right?'

It made a young girl slightly dizzy. To answer his question, I had to put myself in someone else's place, to see the world through their eyes – forgetting what I knew to return to a state of ignorance that I could never have had. Their future, my past. Maybe it was the first test of a writer, and I failed.

Thinking back to that conversation today, I am struck by something else. The reason I assumed people were unaware of the time they were living in had to do with forgetting: I thought the memory of the first war would have been lost to those who lived through it, and even more so to those who hadn't witnessed it but who had been told the tale. I hadn't thought for a second that it was simply because they couldn't imagine a second. To understand the past, I naturally looked backward, whereas I should have been turning my eyes (their eyes) forward.

§

A related observation: we are always in someone else's Middle Ages. At the beginning of the text Plutarch devotes to Theseus in *Parallel Lives* around 100 BCE, he wrote:

As geographers [...] crowd into the edges of their maps parts of the world which they do not know about, adding notes in the margin to the effect that beyond this lies nothing but sandy deserts full of wild beasts, unapproachable bogs, Scythian ice, or a frozen sea, so, in this work of mine, in which I have compared the lives of the greatest men with one another, after passing through those periods which probable reasoning can reach to and real history find a footing in, I might very well say of those that are farther off, Beyond this there is nothing but prodigies and fictions, the only inhabitants are the poets and inventors of fables; there is no credit, or certainty any farther.

Reading these few lines is like reading a description of the year 1000 as one would imagine it today: obscured by legends and inhabited by mythical creatures. As far back as antiquity, the past has been perceived as an era of obscurantism steeping in ignorance and superstition. The edges of maps where all that is found are wild beasts and unapproachable bogs, the line between the known and the unknown, don't exist only in the world of geography: it is the same boundary that separates today from the day before yesterday. Fiction and monsters (a pair brought together by Plutarch) do not only haunt unexplored lands, they are also the people of bygone eras.

Yet, the past is the rock we build our houses on and the ink we write our books with. Sometimes, when we open a door, we find ourselves face to face with a ghost staring back at us, and he is just as scared of us as we are of him. The trick is to take him by the hand, bring him into the light, make him a cup of tea if he wants one, sit down in front of him and paint him until the last one of his shadows has been captured on paper. The ghost may disappear, but the drawing remains.

Similarly, if you bend over an inkwell as you would look into an oil slick, you'll find shapes and colours shimmering in it. You mustn't close your eyes; you need to stay there long enough for shapes to appear. First it is like looking at yourself, like a funhouse mirror. But don't look away. Soon the shadows will appear. They will ask you to dance.

Anna had come to knock on my door a few days before her wedding. As always, she was accompanied by her governess, but rather than escorting her inside, the governess made a gesture with her hand as if to bless her or to warn me before turning on her heel. It was the middle of the night. I thought I was dreaming, and sometimes I still think I was.

She came in smiling and, out of habit, I led her to the atelier, which was bathed in shadow, given the hour. The two portraits were side by side on two easels; I was to relinquish the first one the next morning. She studied them with her fingers in the half-light. Then she said, as if I didn't know, 'I am to be married in three days.'

I agreed in silence.

She went on, 'I have never met the man who is to be my husband, but I am told he is very tall and very rich.' She added, for good measure, 'He is a powerful seigneur.'

Once again I nodded. Had he been deaf, lame and hunchbacked, I still would have been jealous of the man.

It was strange to see her standing facing the two portraits, one of which depicted her as sensible and calm, and the other in the grip of an unseen storm. For a moment, I couldn't tell which of the three Annas was the real one.

She turned around and remarked, 'You're not saying anything.'

'What do you want me to say?'

'We won't see each other again after tomorrow. Are you not in the least bit sad?'

I lurched and, to give the impression of composure, I turned my back on her to go to the window. The houses on the other side of the street were dark. The night was riddled with stars. I heard her move the brushes and paints on my table. When I turned back, she was holding a piece of charcoal.

'I would like to draw your portrait,' she said.

I lit a candle, found a piece of paper, held it out to her.

She sat on the ground and invited me to do the same. Then, the charcoal suspended in the air, she observed me for a long while.

Finally, rather than bringing the tip of the charcoal to the page, she came over to me and delicately traced the arch of my eyebrow, the bone of my nose, the line of my cheek-bone and the curve of my chin, drawing a night mask on my face. With her thumb, she erased a line at the corner of my mouth and then her lips took the place of her finger.

We undressed quietly, in silence, discovering each other with a sort of astonishment. She had an hourglass figure, soft skin and a beauty mark under her left breast, where her heart was. We lay down, arms and legs entwined, under the covers, where I had spent so many nights dreaming of her. When we rose at the hour when the stars go out, our bodies stayed outlined in the folds of the sheets.

§

After her wedding, she still found ways to come see me several times a week. She would arrive laughing, her cheeks red, short of breath; she would settle in close to me like a bird and tell me about the ruses she had used to explain her absence: she had to visit an aunt, a poverty-stricken family, a sick friend; she was going to the market, to the draper, to mass. The last excuse was not entirely an invention, because sometimes she would come join me at Saint Anne's church, where I had agreed to redo the stations of the cross a few months earlier.

She would sit down near me in the deserted nave, watch me work while telling me about her life as the wife of a notable, amusing herself as she would have in a role she might have played in a miracle play. As for her husband, I knew he was rich, naive and arrogant. I did not want to know any more, preferring that he remain a shadow at the edge of my consciousness, like when you spot an indistinct shape out of the corner of your eye without knowing what it is. Most importantly, I did not want to imagine that she could do with him what she continued to do with me – and even once, God forgive us, in the church.

I hadn't seen her for almost ten days when she arrived one morning more excited than usual.

'I had to escape a swarm of cousins – mine and my husband's – who are visiting us for a few days. I snuck away as they were going off to buy lace. They were thrilled about it no end: it will probably be an hour before they realize I am gone.'

She lay her head on my shoulder, her hand on my doublet. We both faced Our Lord staggering under the weight of a cross larger than Him. Dropping my brush and my paints, I took her in my arms. She smelled of the outdoors and the sun.

'What do you do when I'm not here?' she asked.

'I work.'

'And when you're not working?'

'I sleep.'

And when you're not sleeping?'

'I wait.'

It was true. My life was spent in a sort of eternal state of anticipation, but it didn't bother me. I waited for her as one awaits summer, knowing that it will come and that it will be sweet.

Sometimes she brought fruit or thin wafers to share, sometimes a book she would read passages aloud from.

The first time, I was amazed. 'You know how to read?'

'My father didn't have a son.'

My father had four of them, and never enough money to feed them. I was the youngest; I was sent to live with my uncle, my mother's brother, who was the steward of a vast estate in Touraine. He had the use of a large house, along with the stables and forests of a seigneur who rarely stayed there, preferring war to the countryside. I spent part of my childhood there, with his own sons who did not take me into their hearts, except for Robert. He was not much older than me, and he quickly became my defender and best friend.

Generally during these visits, Anna would pull out some needlework she had designed and that she had decorated with brightly coloured threads. That week she had finished a piece of embroidery with a fire-breathing dragon, and now she was busy with a small scene, the lower half of which was underwater. Under the hull of a vessel floating on an ocean dotted with islands lay a scene of sea urchins and seahorses.

I had asked her, somewhat in fun, if she ever embroidered things she had ever seen or met.

She smiled at me. 'Like Saint Veronica and Mary Magdalene?'

She was always smarter than me. But I didn't let up.

'Saint Veronica has your eyes, and Mary Magdalene your smile, as you well know. I have to look at you for hours before I can give them a face.'

I stole a kiss from her. She pulled away.

'Fortunately, sea urchins have no face.'

She ran her thumb over what she had embroidered that day and over the blank fabric left to be stitched. I could see that she was thinking about my question. Her brow was furrowed; she looked like the little girl she must have once been, trying to work out a heavy volume of Carolin-gian minuscule.

'I don't need to recreate what I know,' she finally said. 'Why would I want a copy?'

Months later, Robert explained to me that everything here on earth was already a copy, a pale simulacrum of the true, inexpressible Beauty. But in that moment, I was surprised at Anna's desire to live in a world populated with unicorns and giraffes rather than simply by my side.

And then, like a child who has a toy for the first time in his life and wants to be sure it is his and that no one will take it away, I began to want to test her love for me. When she couldn't come for several days, I greeted her with a sullen face and had to be cajoled before granting her a smile, even though my heart was pounding.

If she told me she could come back Thursday, I would say that I wouldn't be there, even if I had nothing else to do that day but think of her. Did I think my scarcity would increase my value? Or did I simply want her to suffer, just as I suffered every time she left? Driven by a blend of stupidity and cruelty, I even went so far as to invent a rival.

'I've started painting the portrait of a beautiful young lady,' I told her one day when she arrived later than usual.

She started, but asked me in an even voice. 'Will you show it to me?'

I made a face. 'It is far from finished. Maybe in a few weeks. I have to see her again a few times. I have never met anyone with such white skin. A complexion like lilies and roses.'

'Oh, yes?'

'And vermillion lips.'

She was looking at me, taken aback.

I kept going, unable to stop myself, for the nasty pleasure of seeing worry spread across her face. 'Eyes blue as the sea, a flawless profile.'

She stood abruptly, and I held her back to kiss her harder than usual. She stiffened for a moment before kissing me back, and then she left, running through the storm.

She died less than a week later, of a fever, and of course no one came to tell me. I continued to think she was alive for two whole days, and those two days were torture. Had I known right away, I could have taken the road of shadows with her. Twice the sun had come up, twice the moon had been a cradle in the sky – there was no way I could catch up with her.

I went home, took the weld, madder, lamp black and threw the pigments in the fire under the serene gaze of the portrait I was painting at night. Then I fed the flames with the brushes and wood panels I was preparing. I would have thrown my table and chair in the hearth had it been big enough. But no fire was big enough. I clutched her portrait to my chest. The wood was cold and hard. It was no longer her, but stones, shells, roots and bones reduced to powder and mixed with egg yolk spread on what had been a tree – thrown into the fire.

That day, the light went out. The day turned to night, the night turned to ash.

§

First there was blind rage with no words to roar, and I stayed there, mouth open, mute, like a fish out of water. Then the sorrow came crashing down, replaced from time to time by a sort of stupor that was practically a relief. Rage would reappear at the most curious moments. One day I was eating a piece of bread in the street, and a dog started to follow me, begging. I wanted to shoo it away, but the dog wouldn't leave me alone, its dirty muzzle raised toward the crust of bread.

I kicked it without knowing what I was doing. The dog went off, with surprise in its eyes that should have made my heart ache.

§

I fled my atelier, my bed, everything I had shared with her, and that just made her absence more acute. I was looking for places and people that didn't speak to me of her, that were necessarily also the most distant from me. I spent hours roaming the streets. When the sun went down, I would go into an inn, and I would drink until I couldn't stand up. I surrendered to sleep wherever it took me. I slumped in a chair, I crumpled in a doorway or I collapsed in the bony arms of a whore. I would wake with a start a few hours later and head off walking again as if pursued by a ghost.

In spite of all his wisdom, his Greek and his Latin, Robert didn't understand. He had never wanted to die from having lost someone, and no doubt he had no more understanding of wanting to live for a woman. Both of his brothers are married, but to my knowledge they have only ever spoken of their wives in an offhand way, as they offered news of the estate, the harvest and their children. He had definitely never seen them kiss their wives, who were fat, ruddy women, solidly planted in their skirts; it probably would have seemed as ridiculous to him as seeing them seek comfort with farm-yard animals.

He told me that toward the end of his childhood, he had read a few tales of courtly love that made him sigh with pleasure. It wasn't the loves recounted that filled his heart, but the desire to do the same thing – that is, to one day write a book of his own.

He had come to the conclusion that men with similar appearances aren't made the same, like books that look alike containing different truths, or one telling the truth while the other lies. Of two equally red apples, one can have fragrant flesh and the other a worm coiled in its rotting pulp. That is what appearances are like, so it is best to beware.

One day when we were talking about this, he told me, 'There are men who have a stone where their heart should be. I know some like that, and I watch out for them. But others have a heart where their brain should be, and those men are no better.'

§

This morning, at church, I watched the monks, trying to figure out which one needed the poison that is also a remedy. Drawing their portraits, I often had the opportunity to notice that while birds never look like anything but birds, seen under a certain light most men look like birds. With his aquiline nose and deep-set eyes, Brother Louis has the profile of a buzzard. The hair showing around his tonsure is grey, but he always walks with a spring in his step and stands straight. Under the cowls, in the church plunged in shadow, there was a partridge (Brother Thomas, fat and short-limbed, who sounds guttural when he speaks), two crows (Brothers Colin and Maximilien, stern-faced, who look like actual brothers), a pheasant (the tall, fat Brother Alarich, who always seems to be puffing up his throat), a sparrow, a gull, a heron. And Robert? I know him too well to see anything other than the boy he once was – too well or not well enough.

§

For the past few days, at the abbot's table, Brother Adelphe kept going on in praise of the gardens. The vicar, not overly inclined to discuss such coarse matters, tried to feign interest.

'We are pleased with them,' he said, as if he sometimes rose at dawn to plunge his fingers into the earth. 'Not only does the vegetable garden produce enough to feed the brothers, but we can even sell what is leftover to the villagers.'

He appeared to have just realized that it was true: Brother Clément, who could scarcely read and had a hard time following services, produced enough for all of them to eat and brought in money to the abbey. Which goes to show that even the humblest of creatures have their uses. He puffed out his chest.

'No doubt you were the one who suggested the idea to him?' Brother Adelphe asked, to be agreeable.

The vicar seemed to want to neither confirm nor deny and settled for a smile. Brother Louis, seated beside him, stiffened, but Robert looked almost amused by the discussion.

Adelphe continued. 'I have never seen a garden that so perfectly reproduced the impeccable organization of the Abbey of Saint Gall, of course in miniature. There are so few people who manage to recreate it so intelligently. Most settle for drawing inspiration from it, often quite imperfectly, more's the pity, or they think it a good idea to adorn it with whatever they can find.'

This time, the vicar exclaimed, 'Saint Gall, now there's an abbey that must please God! A number of my brothers have stayed there, and I have held the plans in my very own hands.'

While he was saying these words, his voice contained a vexation that he was trying to have pass for admiration –

why wasn't the well-ordered beauty his, for the greater glory of God?

He seemed to be one of those men for whom someone else's success, even fortuitous, inevitably awakened his own sense of failure. Brother Clément's mysterious ability should have brought him contentment, even pride, but what he felt was humiliation. He spent a long time chewing on a mouthful of fresh peas and beans, the success of which depended in no way on him, then he took a glass of wine to wash down the taste.

He had to leave the next day and would be back only in six months, for Christmas.

§

Right after lauds, Robert dragged me around the walls, and we watched the sun come up. In the dawn light, the bay was pink like the inside of a shell. At one time I would have given anything to capture a similar light in painting. Now its beauty is foreign to me. It speaks to me in a forgotten language.

We spotted a group of pilgrims advancing slowly toward the Mont. There must have been sixty of them, maybe more. Oddly, they didn't grow bigger as they approached, as things do when the intervening distance closes in. Or, at least, they weren't growing enough. At one hundred toises from the Mont, they still could have been a miniature army, dirty and tattered, whose soldiers were walking toward the abbey, water up to their ankles. The two in front carried the cross and the pilgrim's staff.

'Who are they?' I asked Robert.

'Children.'

And half under his breath, he recited a song about children flocking to Mont Saint-Michel:

Une M seule, comme semble,
Trois C, trois X, trois I ensemble,
En l'an MCCCXXXIII
A Saint Michiel sa grant fiance
Fist venir au mont grantentois
De pastoreaus grant habundance.

One hundred years later, the little pilgrims were once again on the road to paradise.

The horde of little boys went through the King's Gate in a long, straggly line and entered the village on a slope. They started the climb toward the abbey by the Grand Degré, in silence, determined. Their light steps pattered on the cobblestones like rain.

I followed Robert and entered into the almonry, where the little pilgrims had assembled and were undressing. Some were already lying on the ground, others eating pieces of bread that had been brought in deep baskets. You could hear buzzing in several languages and dialects. Robert addressed one of the taller children, standing not far away, with gangly limbs and brown hair, who could have been twelve years old.

'Are you the leader?' he asked in the Norman dialect.

'We don't have a leader,' the child answered.

'Very well. Who was walking in front?' Robert asked.

The child pointed to the middle of the crowd, where a little boy of around eight, red-haired like a fox, was busy unpacking his meagre luggage. Clearing a path through the children, we approached him.

'What is your name?' Robert asked softly.

The little boy raised his head but didn't answer. He had pure green eyes, lined with red lashes, and a solemn look.

His pupils seemed almost liquid. He had red lips and cheeks dotted with freckles.

'Where have you come from?' I tried in turn.

More silence.

The expression on the boy's face made me think he might be deaf. I asked in a slightly louder voice, enunciating clearly, 'Can you hear what I'm saying?'

The child lifted his palms to the sky and mumbled something we didn't understand. But Robert recognized the lilt of his words: it was German. Turning back to the older boy, he ordered him to come act as interpreter.

'Please forgive me, Abbot, sir, I can't.'

'Why on earth not?'

'I don't speak German, sir.'

'All right. One of the others must understand it, no?'

'Oh, yes, several of them.'

'Very well, so bring me one. He can serve as interpreter.'

'It's just that…'

'Yes?'

'They don't speak Norman, sir.'

'How in heaven's name did you manage to understand each other if you all speak different dialects?'

The boy opened his eyes wide, as if the question had never occurred to him. Robert nodded his head and smiled a little in spite of himself.

'It seems that what God took from man in Babel,' he whispered to me, shaking his head, 'he gave to these little children.'

Fortunately there was a monk at Mont Saint-Michel who had spent a great deal of time at the Alpirsbach Abbey, and had come here to study works from the last century that dealt with mathematics. Robert sent for him. Around him, the children were still resting. The room had become one big camp. Children were playing dice in a corner. Others were already snoring. The little redhead hardly spoke to the others, but they glanced at him from time to time as if to make sure he was still there.

Brother Alarich finally arrived, and Robert asked the child again, 'What is your name?' which Brother Alarich translated into a slightly guttural-sounding language of which I didn't understand a word.

'Johann,' the child said.

'And where have you come from?'

The child shrugged.

'Did he understand the question?' Robert asked Brother Alarich, who repeated it, more slowly.

'He says he doesn't know,' Alarich translated once the child answered.

'He doesn't know where he came from?'

'That's what he said.'

Robert tried a different approach: 'What cities did you travel through to get here?'

'A few big cities and many hamlets. In some places, people gave us food and let us sleep in haylofts, or even in the kitchen, near the hearth. In other places, they chased us off.' As if to alleviate the sting of his words, he added, 'But that didn't happen often.'

When the brother had finished translating, Robert continued, 'How long did you walk for?'

'Days and moons. We left in the spring to arrive in the summer.'

'How did you know which way to go?'

'The Sun guided my feet.'

'And now that you are here?'

'I would like to speak to the angel, please.'

That evening, after the service, Robert came to find me in my cell. He had ended up giving me a space just big enough for a straw mattress, with a narrow window, after the monks in the neighbouring beds complained that I would get up in the middle of the night and disrupt their sleep. One's sleep must be bad indeed to be accused of bothering men who rise every three hours to pray. I was stretched out on the straw, with my eyes open, my mind blank. I sat up when I saw him come in. He took the small book with the worn cover and rounded corners from his cowl. I recognized it as the book he had brought back from our journey and not shown the vicar. He opened it to the first page and asked me, 'Do you know what that says?'

'I don't read Latin,' I answered curtly, as if he didn't know. I wanted to say, or didn't want to say, 'You know I don't know how to read.'

'It's Greek,' Robert continued softly.

He flipped through the book and stopped at a left-hand page covered with illuminations. 'Could you do this?' he asked me.

I studied the cinnabar-red and emerald-green drawings that were crude and a little clumsy, in spite of the gold that bordered them.

'I could do better than that,' I answered.

It wasn't vanity; it was true.

Robert clarified the misunderstanding. Pointing to the right-hand page with a forest of small characters that appeared under a large dropped initial, he asked me, 'And what about that? Could you do that too?'

I can draw my name at the bottom of a bill or a painting; that has always been enough. I don't know how to read or write, but that has not bothered me. What I know of books are the tales Anna read me. Since coming to Mont Saint-Michel, I have visited the scriptorium a few times with Robert, who had me admire the illuminations and run my finger over the grain of the parchment or the vellum. I contemplated the colourful dropped initials with some interest, as one would look at a forest of plants whose names and fragrances are unfamiliar. Brother Louis initially flat out refused to let me rummage through the books in the library, arguing that they were not meant to be sullied by profane hands. When Robert explained what he had in mind, the old man actually jumped.

'Never!'

Robert patiently explained, 'But he knows ink and parchment as well if not better than our young monks. And there are undoubtedly things he could teach them on handling a quill.'

'I am not denying that he may be skilled at playing with brushes. But have you at least considered, in your wisdom, that he does not understand the truth that is revealed in these pages when he can't decipher even the first letter?'

They were talking about me as if I weren't there, and, in truth, I felt as though I wasn't completely there. This wasn't my plan; Brother Louis's objections didn't bother me. He might be right: these books were precious, definitely not treasures you would put in just anyone's hands. Through the window, I was watching two white birds circling. I couldn't tell which was pursuing which, or if they were performing a sort of dance. At the other end of the room, I could hear their conversation without really listening to it. They would tell me the verdict soon enough.

'And who can claim to understand the words of the saints and, more importantly, those of Our Lord in their entirety, even if he can decipher the next twenty-five letters?' Robert replied.

Brother Louis seemed caught off-guard for a moment.

'And anyway, what does that change?' Robert continued.

'What does that change?'

Brother Louis was choking a little. I glanced in their direction. His cheeks were turning pink. It was as though he had made a great effort and was out of breath. And he was in fact making a great effort: not to explode in rage.

'Is it the duty of our monks to judge what they are copying?' Robert continued.

'No, of course not.'

Brother Louis's cheeks were still red, and the flush was spreading to his neck, leaving blotches on the white skin.

'You would never suggest that it is up to them to change it in any way whatsoever, would you?'

When this possibility was raised, Brother Louis flinched. 'On the contrary, we need to preserve the truth as is and unchanged,' he said in a hushed voice. 'To convey it intact for the edification of centuries to come. To keep it from all those who are not worthy of receiving it.'

'And who chooses who is worthy?'

Brother Louis raised his eyes to the heavens, either to answer the question or to beg help from above.

'The sacred texts must be kept by men of God in sacred places. Infidel texts must be kept in the same place, but for other reasons; their noxious influence must be stopped from spreading.' Raising his finger, he spoke as if he were reading from an invisible book. 'The former must be protected from the wicked; the innocent must be protected from the latter.'

Robert interrupted him as if he had caught him out, but when he began speaking it was as though he were trying to convince Brother Louis that they were in agreement, that they were saying the same thing in different words.

'Precisely,' he explained. 'The texts that we must protect ourselves from, perhaps they would better be copied by someone who will not fall under their corrupting influence? As for those that proclaim the divine truth, they ask only to be transcribed and copied. What can it matter if one is mute, deaf or blind, so long as one has agile hands. And I do not know anyone with fingers as agile as Éloi's.'

Brother Louis ended up giving in. Not because he had run out of arguments, I'm sure, or because he had been convinced by Robert's – I could see in his eyes that that wasn't the case. But he seemed to have understood that one cannot win through reason against someone who has decided on madness.

The next day, he set up a work table for me in the scriptorium, which was deserted. On the tabletop, with precise gestures full of reverence, he laid two duck quills, a knife for sharpening them, a compass, a reed pen, a long ruler, a silver nib and a scraper. Then he laid before me a single well, half-filled with black ink.

'We won't need any colour today,' he ordained, and I did not try to contradict him.

He went away and came back with parchment already covered with half-erased writing.

'You need to clean it before you can use it again,' he said.

I scraped that entire day and part of the next morning, managing to get some of the remaining characters to disappear. But others were still visible, and I was afraid, in continuing to rub, that I would make a hole in the delicate surface. Brother Louis put an end to my concerns.

'That will do.'

I wondered whether I was supposed to draw my letters over the old ones to try to cover them or put them in the spaces between the lines of the text that had half disappeared, only a ghost of it remaining. I chose the latter. When Brother Louis came to see how I was doing, he seemed to approve, even though he didn't say so. He settled for walking away nodding his head.

But the result looked curious to me, since I was not in the habit of writing: the new characters drawn in black ink alternated with almost invisible lines, but the paleness between the letters made them stand out even more. And it is true that one needed to be more attentive to make them out than to follow the new lines, which jumped out at you. Nonetheless, they ended up intertwining such that the two texts, which should have been foreign to one another, appeared to be one.

In the seventeenth century, the Maurists who had arrived at Mont Saint-Michel to succeed the Benedictines inscribed in the library's volumes the now famous ex-libris *Ex monasterio sancti Michaelis in periculo mari – From the monastery of Saint Michel at peril from the sea*, even though the library and scriptorium's days of glory were long behind them, and only two or three books were copied in it each year.

During the Revolution, the saints and their corteges of archangels left, and Mont Saint-Michel was rebaptized Mont Michel, and then Mont Libre. And, in an ironic fate, the abbey was officially converted to a prison; most of the prisoners were neither criminals of common law nor aristocrats, but rather priests accused of not embracing revolutionary values fervently enough.

A strange reversal, from cloister to prison – both places to be shut away, the former voluntary, the latter involuntary. The difference between these two types of confinement is the same as that between marriage for love and the act of rape. In the one case, something is given; in the other, something is taken.

§

In 1834, the abbey's divided church, separated by a floor at mid-height meant to increase the usable area, became a hat workshop. Two years later, in a letter to his daughter Adèle, Victor Hugo writes of a visit to Mont Saint-Michel:

> *In the château, there is the sound of bolts, the sound of tradesmen, shadows that watch shadows that work [...], the wonderful Knights Hall, which has been turned into a workshop where through a skylight one can see ghastly grey*

men bustling about, looking like enormous spiders, the Romanesque nave turned into a squalid refectory, the charming cloister with such delicate arches transformed into a shabby promenade, [...] everywhere the dual degradation of man and monument feeding off one another. That is present-day Mont Saint-Michel.

And then, to replace the angel torn from the bell tower, the simulacrum of a cross:

The crowning glory, at the top of the pyramid, at the spot where the huge golden statue of the archangel shone, four black sticks are fretting. It's the telegraph.

§

In 1878–1879, a causeway was erected leading to Mont Saint-Michel on which a train ran until 1938. A few years later, images of Mont Saint-Michel under the Occupation brought to mind dystopias where you saw the latest in dirigibles floating over the familiar silhouette of New York skyscrapers. In another universe, which resembled ours in almost every respect, men sported the swastika, filled cattle trains with terrified men, women and children, built camps the size of cities where the ovens burned night and day. They marched through Europe, took Mont Saint-Michel and occupied the abbey.

A forest's worth of piles were planted in the sludge to prevent ships from sailing into the bay. They were nicknamed Rommel's asparagus. One would have thought the Mont during the Occupation would have resembled a stronghold or a strategic position, with watches and rounds, guards on every corner. It was nothing like that. The baker continued to bake his bread, Mother Poulard to whip her eggs; there may have been fewer tourists, although that is not certain. Essentially, nothing had changed, and one can't help but think that the most atrocious thing was not the aberration of death trains, gas ovens, madmen and sadists. No, the most atrocious thing was the quiet normalcy of good people eating an omelette in the midst of the horror.

§

Today the causeway leads to a large parking lot at the base of the ramparts. A new army, in metal and chrome, has laid siege to the abbey. Morning till night, buses line up in tight rows, gleaming in the sun. For the past few years there has been a great deal of fuss around dismantling the causeway, which is responsible for the bay silting up, and which will be replaced by a bridge on stilts, allowing the water to circulate freely. After five hundred and fifty years, Mont Saint-Michel will become an island once more. It will have beaten back the invaders yet again.

§

The silhouette of Mont Saint-Michel as we know it today dates back to 1898, when the abbey was crowned with the spire from which the archangel Michael rises, striking down the dragon of the Apocalypse.

The statue is the work of Emmanuel Frémiet, who learned his craft in the macabre workshops of the morgue, where painters touched up cadavers that were decomposing or that had other defects that would be shocking to see. Frémiet is known mainly for his animal subjects, including bronzes of Napoleon's basset hounds and a curious statue of a gorilla kidnapping a half-naked woman, seeming to foreshadow King Kong.

The statue of the archangel made for Mont Saint-Michel's spire is nothing if not traditional: sword raised, shield brandished in front of him, Michael, with a crown on his head and dressed in a coat of mail, rests his foot on a sort of large fish representing the dragon, which is supposed to signify evil. I would forget, because they seemed almost to vanish, obscured by the realism of the statue, but on Michael's back there is a pair of large golden wings.

We learned more through snatches of information from the children. They were mostly around ten years old. The youngest one seemed barely six or seven. The first ones left from Germany, around Thuringia. Their numbers swelled as they advanced, like a snowball growing as it rolls. Many didn't know where they were walking to. Others had such an intense desire to see the archangel Michael that they left in spite of their parents having forbidden it. One of the smallest had fled through his bedroom window at night to join the others. There was a story that a newborn had begged his mother to let him leave and that she was so astonished to hear him speak that she dropped him on the floor. The children walked morning till night, in the direction of the setting sun. Some chanted:

In Gottes Namen fahren wir,
Zu Sankt Michael woollen wir!

Most said nothing.

§

At the end of the day, there is not much light in the scriptorium. We toil like shadows amid shadows, hoods up. Sometimes I stop to listen to the scratching of the quills on the vellum, trying to imagine the birds the large feathers were snatched from and the dead calves in the womb of the cow, skinned so that we can write on their hides, and I am astonished that something that resembles life could emerge from so much death. In front of me, on the white surface, the letters appear one by one, like fish plucked from the depths.

Brother Louis still purses his lips when I sit down at my table and take up my quill, and I do not know if it is a sign that he disapproves of my presence in the scriptorium or whether he thinks the book I'm copying is not worthy of the effort. But it is not his to choose, and his disapproval is no doubt great enough to encompass both the codex and me.

Nevertheless, he seems to be getting used to me working at his side. This morning, he had me admire a page in a book he was looking through that showed two animals with horse bodies, each one with a horn on the front. They seemed to be clashing.

'I didn't know unicorns fought one another,' I said.

He looked at me with a mix of pity and disdain. 'Those aren't unicorns,' he answered, as if it were obvious. 'They are monoceroses. More massive, more aggressive.'

The animals did have a stronger breast than one would normally see on a unicorn. But still, how could you tell the difference? When I asked him, the disdain disappeared from his eyes, replaced by pity: 'It is written.'

The pages of the book contained every animal under creation and many more still: weasels, whales, basilisks, centaurs, civets and caladri. I sometimes thought I recognized an animal or a bird, but Brother Louis quickly corrected me when I was mistaken.

I stopped before an expansive scene showing some ten winged creatures of different sizes and colours, gathered around a well. Among those drawn in great detail, one of the largest had a semicircular object in its beak. Noticing that I was studying it, Brother Louis said, 'It's an ostrich.'

'Where is that written?' I asked this time, not seeing letters anywhere on the page or on the next one.

'It is not written. But it is holding a horseshoe in its beak.' Seeing me perplexed, he explained, 'The ostrich is known for its iron stomach and can swallow anything, which is why it is often shown with a horseshoe in its beak.'

I raised my eyes, thinking. So, to understand books, you didn't just need to know how to decipher the letters; you had to know how to read what wasn't written.

§

That morning, he had me admire ornamental letters in an old book entitled *Moralia in Job*, showing me what was special about it.

'The monks at the time had respect for sacred texts,' he sniffed. 'It wasn't like today, when anyone can claim to be a scribe, and the workshops in the cities are filled with bad painters scribbling little scenes instead of reading the Holy Scriptures.'

He didn't seem to realize that I was precisely one of those painters, or else he just didn't care if he offended me.

'The ornamental letters were designed here at a time when books were still books and not garish daubs,' he told me, before showing me a large, remarkable P that was almost as tall as the page.

I looked at him, incredulous.

'The monks created their own alphabet?'

He almost smiled. 'No, not their alphabet, but their way of drawing it, which was specific to certain regions, or even, like here, certain abbeys. These letters are from Mont Saint-Michel. Look: the contour is straight and masterful,' he pointed out, and it was true. 'There is rich intertwining, which is an old tradition here – and then there are acanthi.'

Seeing me perplexed, he patiently explained: 'Branches that leaves, flowers and fruit spring out of, that grow from the main stem. And living creatures hide in the branches.'

And indeed, in the head of the P, a man armed with an axe was threatening a wildcat. The wildcat, its mouth wide open, was trying to bite the leaves. Most of the letter was in a rich blue rimmed with red and embellished with green. A few details were traced in blackish-brown or lilac, which you wouldn't notice unless you were studied the drop cap with attention. The effect was not only harmonious but also singularly evocative.

'Who did this?' I asked him, admiring the work.

The librarian shrugged.

'We don't know anymore. This book dates back over five centuries. This brother has not been with us for a long time, and his name has been forgotten.'

'So it doesn't appear anywhere?'

'No. It's not good for a monk to get too attached to the fruit of his labour. You know the Rule.'

Realizing that he was not speaking to a young monk but to a man who was not as familiar with it as he was, he recited from memory: 'If there are artisans in the monastery, let them practice their crafts with all humility, provided the Abbot has given permission. But if any one of them becomes conceited over his skill in his craft, because he seems to be conferring a benefit on the monastery, let him be taken from his craft.'

I looked at him without understanding. I ended up asking, 'But, Brother, why take his craft away from him if he excels at it for the glory of the monastery?'

'For a number of reasons, each of which is reason enough. First because he is breaking the first rule, which is to be humble. No one should think he has value aside from what is lent to him by our Lord Almighty. And because he is also breaking his vow of poverty.'

I was understanding less and less, as was often the case with these monks; they confused when they were trying to enlighten.

'But that brother isn't selling the fruit of his labour...' I ventured.

'No, but he believes that the work belongs to him, when no brother may own anything.'

'Not even talent.'

'Especially not talent. The rule does not say that you have to be humble, but that you have to become humble. That means that every day must be used to slay one's pride and flee the causes of it.'

'And therefore, there is always something to slay. And something to flee,' I said under my breath, not knowing whether my words went unheard or he simply chose to ignore them.

Cautiously turning the thick sheets, he was still admiring the exquisite marginalia that had lost none of its brilliance in five centuries. The monk who had done it was dead, forever excised, but the images were still coming to life before the eyes and under the fingers of an unknown brother. The drawing on the page knew nothing of pride, it only knew the colour of it.

On the beach, at the base of the rock, two children are looking out at the expanse of grey, trying to make out in the distance where the sea ends and the sky begins. The line is invisible, and it surrounds us. They arrived a few days ago, and they are leaving tomorrow.

'How is it,' the smallest one asked, scanning the water, 'that you never see the sea serpents that sailors talk about?'

The boy's father was a fisherman, and a lover of legends, before he died needlessly from the pox.

"They stay at the very edge of the sea to condemn fool-hardy ships to the depths,' the oldest one explained.

The little one shuddered. 'And giant octopuses, and narwhals?'

'Narwhals live near the islands. And octopuses, maybe they don't exist.'

'Oh.'

He would have liked to have seen these strange sea creatures but is almost as happy to imagine them, as he stands, feet in the water, in the shadow of the stone fortress that took one hundred days to reach. They weren't sure *it* existed before getting here.

Sometimes, you don't really have to believe; you just have to keep walking.

§

They had walked through countries, forests and villages. The youngest one had no family. The day he started his journey, he left a farmer and his wife who had been giving him room and board – cold gruel in a draughty hayloft – in exchange for his work in the fields. He hadn't given them a second thought, but he missed the cows.

The oldest was in fact the youngest of a litter of delinquents living in the city with their sick mother. As a young boy he had learned to steal and lie. He too had left with a light heart when he saw a group of children go on their way to visit an angel in the middle of the water. He had always dreamed of seeing the ocean.

They had become friends quickly, wordlessly. The oldest one helped the youngest through the difficult parts; the little one showed the oldest which leaves were edible. They called the older one Andreas and the younger one Casimir. For the past few days, Casimir had been coughing so much he sometimes had to stop to catch his breath. Andreas would stop too and, not knowing what else to do, pray in a soft voice.

That night the little one lost consciousness and was rushed to the infirmary. Through the narrow window, he tried to see the statue of the angel, but could see only the clouds forming, drawing snakes and winged horses, then breaking up and dissipating just as quickly, and then the stars starting to spiral in the dark. It was like seeing sparkling fish dancing in the night sky. Soon, exhausted, he stopped opening his eyes.

Cape Elizabeth, Maine, again, we spend our days on a deserted white-sand beach, right near Richmond Island, the outline of which we can see from the shore. This vast, practically wild territory has belonged to the same wealthy family since the nineteenth century; there are a few stately homes, a smattering of stables and barns, fields, prairies and forests, a few ponds and a cemetery that I have never seen. At sundown we see deer; a rabbit watches us as we head home, while in the high grass families of turkeys and pheasants waddle about. We watch ducks and geese take flight. These lands are just as they were five hundred years ago, indifferent to our presence. The beasts tolerate us because we are not very imposing as guests.

On the beach, we collect sand dollars by the dozens, pale little discs marked with the seal of a star that as a child I believed with all my heart was mermaid money. With water up to my knees, I bend over and come back up holding a spiral shell bigger than a fist, faded white and lilac. A sharp, brownish shell is lightly drifting around my toes, rising, shooting off, then a second one, then a third. Soon dozens of hermit crabs are rushing around in silence in the current.

This long, deserted beach has two sections separated by a jetty of rocks that leads to the islands where sheep graze. The paper we are handed when we arrive at the house we have rented says that you are allowed to go to the island by boat, and even to pitch a tent, but that you are not allowed to gather anything or build a fire; it ends with this admonition: *Please do not harass the sheep*. The sheep that must not be harassed have one of the most beautiful views on the East Coast.

Unmoved when I present her with enormous mussel shells with their purple nacre inside, clams as big as my hand, rosaries of green algae, my daughter is ecstatic when she finds the smallest of twigs, a dead leaf, another dead leaf in the yellowed grass. She spends hours on the beach filling and emptying her bucket. The grains of sand are as fine as powder in an hourglass, ash blond, moon dust. I realize that that's what I want to give her: a sandcastle, her house by the sea.

We arrive at the beach at the end of a labyrinth in the forest snaked with rutted, narrow dirt roads: one crosses a pine forest that smells like rosemary; another crosses groves of lacy ferns that pierce the sun's rays. For a moment, we drive around a large pond where ducks and geese float among the water lilies; elsewhere, we discover the remains of an orchard where at dusk the deer eat apples right from the trees. In a field, in the long grass, there lies a beached rowboat, open to the elements. And then at the end of the labyrinth in the forest, a path of grey planks set over a swamp begins. We walk at the height of cattails, among dragonflies and the song of the cicadas; we cross a long green arbour, and the dunes begin, the planks climb and seem to stop in the middle of the sky. Beyond that is the sea. It is here, right here, that I want to live.

In writing this sentence, I first mistakenly put down *write* rather than *live*, and that is true too.

§

The French word for *novel*, *roman*, comes from a word used for an early dialect of French, called *Romance*, derived from the popular *langue d'oïl*, which in the Middle Ages stood in opposition to Latin, the language of science and the elite. One spoke to God in Latin, one spoke of love in Romance. It was the language of lullabies, laughter and secrets. It still is.

It is said of the Romance dialect that it was a 'natural' language, reminiscent of the Adamic language postulated by some. So there are languages that come from the outside (Greek, Latin, dictated by God), and other languages, innate, that do not need to be learned. Languages that come down from on high, a language that springs from the ground – *Adam*, in Hebrew, means *clay*.

And yet the novel, *le roman*, as a literary form, has only existed since the sixteenth century. It was born with *Don Quixote*. It could have died there, and we wouldn't have lost that much in the process, that first work being so absolute. But, strangely, that first novel is also already a sort of *mise en abyme*, or Droste effect, because it tells of the adventures of an old man from La Mancha who, his head filled with mythical exploits from having read too many knight's tales, ends up believing he is a knight. He puts on a rusty sallet, mounts a skinny mare and sets off to fight windmills for a lady of the night.

Cervantes and Shakespeare never met, but they both died on April 23, 1616. This is why April 23 is World Book Day. But the fact that at the beginning of the seventeenth century Spain had already adopted the Gregorian calendar, while England was still using the Julian calendar, was overlooked. The two greatest authors who ever lived indeed died on the same date, but ten days apart. It's what you might call a problem of translation.

I long sought to understand why Mont Saint-Michel had made such an impression on me. It is majestic, of course, sovereign, grand; but why was its discovery tied up in my mind with the need to write or, more precisely, the possibility of writing? (During the first trip, I bought a notebook with my allowance that I diligently started to fill.) It was because for the first time, I had arrived on the island of books. It existed. I could live there.

I could spend years exploring the few laneways of Mont Saint-Michel without beginning to understand the mystery of the first stone. Maybe the solution lies there: finding that first stone, shattering it to look inside, to the beginning of the ages. In the meantime, one thousand years ago men created lace out of granite to climb up to God. Others came to the foot of the church to build their village, raise their children, bury their dead.

This place seems to be screaming something at me that I don't understand: that I lived here in another life or that I will in my next one, that I should have been a cloistered nun there, that I have been a scribe, a pilgrim, a horse galloping slower than the tide, a hermit, a cockle fishermen, a sandy sailor, Mother Poulard, a bishop with a hole in his head, an archangel or a bull chained to a post. Who can say?

§

One didn't become a monk in the fifteenth century for the same reasons that one joins an order today. At the time, the decision had social, cultural, economic and political meaning, whereas now it is essentially a personal choice. Back then, the youngest of the family, who knew he had no inheritance and whose older brothers had taken up arms in service of their king, their duke or their seigneur, would become a monk. It was also a way of living comfortably and occasionally having influence, while gaining access to heaven and, if needed, a pass for one's loved ones – spouses and children included, because sometimes the vow of chastity and poverty was interpreted more broadly.

But the reasons for setting out on a pilgrimage haven't changed: hope and hopelessness. For a thousand years, people have walked to get away from or to find something. (*Something* can mean consolation, illumination, peace, God or oneself.) To advance toward a goal, no matter how distant and inaccessible. To impose a tangible trial on oneself and one's faith, of distance covered, suffering and cold. For pain to win out over doubt. To pray with something other than one's lips, for the whole body – bruised feet, dirty hands, tired legs, heart pulsing in the veins – to become a prayer machine.

We tend to think that monasteries are built in isolated places that are hard to get to so as to put distance between the monks and the distractions and temptations of the world, but what if that were just a secondary reason? What if they were built at the top of abrupt peaks, at the bottom of caves dug in the side of a mountain or, like here, in the middle of the ocean, first and foremost to test the faith of pilgrims? Because anyone who builds this sort of sanctuary is not building a place – a destination – but is tracing the route that leads there. The monastery is not the goal, as one might believe, but simply a step that marks the mid-point, because as soon as pilgrims arrive they have to turn around to leave (unless they become monks themselves or die there). They have to go through the same obstacles in reverse, but this time they present an additional risk: they have to add boredom to the dangers posed by steep walls and quicksand. The route is no longer fresh. They are not straining with the desire to reach the holy place. They leave that behind them. How do people leave Mont Saint-Michel?

While pilgrims to Santiago de Compostela proudly wear the convex, striated Santiago shell, full as the moon, pilgrims to Mont Saint-Michel make do with the humble limpet in the shape of a cone, so common in the region that the sand is studded with them at low tide. While there are many stalls that sell them – often deep into the countryside – pilgrims have to find their own shell; it is the mark and the sign of their journey. When they leave Mont Saint-Michel, they take with them a piece of curved shell, a small cathedral that smells of the sea and that echoes its whisper.

Perhaps I was being punished for having wanted to represent life – the sin of idolatry combined with that of pride. Just like the arrogant Hebrews grovelling before the golden calf they had made. That became clear to me this morning. Only a madman can look the sun in the eyes. I was worse than mad: I was in love and I was jealous.

That week they were reading Exodus at the refectory. I asked Brother Clément, who was seated beside me, to translate, which he did, in a hushed voice, and his words were etched into my brain.

> *'Thou shalt not make unto thee any graven image, or any likeness of any thing that is in heaven above, or that is in the earth beneath, or that is in the water under the earth.'*

So after that list, what is left, except for the fantastic creatures Anna filled her tapestries with? They belong neither to the realm of the heavens nor the earth; most were woven from her imagination. So these were the only monsters that would not offend God? Why was she struck down, if she did not sin? Would it not have been more fair that she live and I die?

Her ghost still walks beside me. Reaching out my arm, I see the black shadow of her hand on the ground. Her silence answers my words, and in moments when I still lift my eyes to the heavens, I see nothing more than an abyss and its gaping blue mouth.

Some men are born to build cathedrals to celebrate God, others to build bridges to cross rivers or write books to record the wisdom of the ages. All of this is right, no doubt. As for me, I wanted to commit beauty to a panel of wood as one would pin a butterfly to fabric, not realizing that, to do this, first you must kill it.

§

Back when she would secretly come to find me in my atelier, Anna would watch me work with the same curiosity as if she were watching a bird make its nest. She studied my powders and lacquers, watched me mix oil, egg yolk and pigments to achieve the colour I wanted, not asking any questions, but following each of my gestures.

'Why does this interest you so much?' I asked her one day.

'Because it's what you love.'

And then, as she often loved words more than things, she got it into her head to rename the colours as I spread them on my palette. Her favourites were named *grasshopper*, *breadcrumbs*, *liver*, *egret*, *gingiva*, *cattail*, *twilight*.

For months I have surrounded myself with only grey, a colourlessness that has no name.

What I know of words she taught me. She collected them, some for their sound and some for their meaning, as one collects pebbles for their colour or because they feel smooth in the hand.

Most of the words I know and use rather awkwardly to talk about the world around me, I owe to her. I never went to school, and I was never considered worthy of a conversation on any serious topic. But in reading to me, Anna was not just telling me a story with words, she was also telling me the story of the words, as if they were characters in a tale: where they came from, what their different forms were, who their family was, how they got to where she found them. I enjoyed repeating these new words. Still today, when one comes to my lips, for an instant I feel as if I have found her again.

Occasionally, she asked me whether I wanted to learn to read. I told her no: I am not scholarly enough, I am too lazy. The truth is that I wanted words to be hers so as not to miss the pleasure I felt when she gave them to me.

That afternoon, two whole tree trunks were burning in the huge fireplace, but my fingers were still stiff from the cold. From time to time, I would get up to walk a little, stamping my feet, clapping my hands, blowing into my palms, which I held over the flames until they started to tingle, and then I would sit back down. There were only three of us working on these very cold days. Brother David, who had arrived a few months earlier from the Poblet Monastery in Spain, was taking notes for a translation he had been assigned there. Colin was busy copying a book so old that it almost turned to dust every time he turned a page. Now he was rushing, and the characters he was drawing on the parchment weren't as regular.

Brother Louis was sitting a little ways away, near the large cabinets that housed the books and that only he and Robert had the key to. I didn't know whether books were normally kept this way in the room we were working in, but sometimes their presence made me uncomfortable. Just like in the ossuary, surrounded by the skulls of dead monks, I felt like I was being watched.

Robert came to check on my progress, and I took the opportunity to ask him a question that had been bothering me for some time without my being able to put it into words.

'The other day you said that the text by Aristarchus of Samos told us little about the world, but a great deal about us...,' I began.

'That's not quite what I said.'

'But...'

'I said that not being able to tell whether it contained truth or lies says little about him and a lot about us. The candle does not light itself: its light reveals what is around it.'

'Very well,' I continued, determined to ask him the question that had formed in my mind over the course of the hours spent transcribing the book. 'So what about that other book you presented to Vicar Thibaud, the one that tells the story of Charlemagne's false pilgrimage?'

He smiled the smile that came to him when he intended to answer a question with a question. 'How can you say that it is not the true pilgrimage of a fake Charlemagne instead?' he asked.

'Precisely, I don't know. What does the book – which does not even claim to tell the truth – teach us about the world, or about ourselves?'

Robert was silent for a moment, and then said, 'About the world as it is, not much. But about us, it says something very important, and says it not by saying it but by showing it, because it is itself the proof: mathematics, philosophy, even faith' – and in saying this, he crossed himself, which he did not often do, and so the gesture struck me – 'are not sufficient for man.'

He was right, but, if my life had depended on it, I never would have known what was missing from his list of the useful, the true and the divine. He looked away from me, and I thought he didn't have the answer either, or in any case, he would not tell me what it was. But that's when he whispered, 'It is not enough for us to learn, to know and to believe. We still have to invent.'

I had put down my quill to listen to him; I was looking distractedly in front of me at the wells that contained the inks we mixed with powders kept in shells at Mont Saint-Michel. We remained silent for a moment, and then, indicating the ink, he continued, 'They all look black, don't they?'

It was true: in spite of the large round windows, once it was past noon, there was no real light in the large room, and the inks all looked mysterious and dark.

'You have to dip your quill in them and place the tip on the parchment before you can see the red, emerald or blue that are contained there, invisible in the dark, like the original night from which the Creator drew the light,' Robert explained.

I couldn't help but smile on hearing this thought. It takes a monk to find God in an inkwell.

'Alas, far from growing lighter, some things become more mysterious with time. What we thought we knew at age twenty is muddled and blurred at age forty, as if life were just a long journey in a forest where the path, at first clearly traced, gradually fades and then splits in two, starts to take loops and twists and turns, then disappears altogether, only to reappear where we were not looking for it, doubled this time, both branches gradually separating from one another, each becoming one hundred branches, just like the main branches of a tree divide until they become so fragile they can hold only the weight of a bird – and all this time the light is fading.'

He stopped to catch his breath. I looked at him, surprised. This dark mood wasn't like him, or in any case it wasn't like him to share it this way. But he went on, in a voice that was breaking, 'Yet shouldn't it be the reverse? Shouldn't we go from ignorance to knowledge and from the dark to the light?'

His voice had dropped to a whisper. At that moment, his eyes seemed to have truly lost the ability to see the light; he had the fixed stare of the blind. I am not used to this sort of discussion and never before had anyone spoken to me that way. But I knew what it was like to live surrounded by shadows.

'And if we had to learn to do without light, to tame the night?' I said after a moment. 'A friend told me once that the secret was just to stay upright and keep walking.'

These words seemed to draw him out of his thoughts. He stared at me as if he was astonished to find me there beside him and offered a weak smile. I noticed that there were shadows under his eyes, but it may have just been the fading day. He was slightly stooped, his hands on his stomach like a man who didn't feel well. Looking at the lines recently added between the old lines on the parchment before me, I wondered whether, since the beginning of time, only one book existed, which we were all working on without realizing it.

When Robert left, his step on the flagstones was as light as a bird's.

§

That night, we were awakened by a storm as violent as any I have ever seen. The rain came down in black sheets, split only by lightning. Waves like walls hurled themselves against the bottom of the ramparts, and everywhere you could hear the wind howl. The monks prayed in silence to the light of candles. And then lightning struck the church again – the new part, still unfinished, without damaging a single stone. The monks saw it as a sign of protection from the archangel Michael, a messenger between heaven and earth, in this sanctuary that bears his name. As for me, I'm not so sure. But during the storm I realized that I am not afraid of lightning; it is the rain that alarms me, a thousand fingers snapping at once, the thunder echoing them. I am not afraid of fire, but I am of water.

Today, the little boys left like a cloud of sparrows. They arrived as small adults; they leave as children. Perhaps it is a miracle of the angel they had come to visit. Only two stayed behind: a little boy named Andreas, who is still watching over a younger one, named Casimir, who has had a fever since their arrival and who has been moved to the infirmary where I visit him every day.

The sleeping child speaks an invented language in his dreams, flailing his arms and legs as if he were swimming. Every time he throws off his blanket, I pull it up under his chin. For a few minutes, he is calm. His chest rises and falls regularly. And then another wave comes over him. He starts to move again, he battles phantom monsters, his forehead drenched in sweat. I don't know whether I should try to calm him again or wake him up. There are nights when it is unclear where rest will come from.

To calm him, I started softly singing a lullaby that I must have heard as a child but that I don't recall remembering. I couldn't remember half the words, and I settled for humming the melody. The child continued to flail, but his movements slowed. After a time, he too was humming in his dream. Our voices rose up in the night. Around us, the stars and the fish went quiet to hear us. Perhaps it was their way of singing.

The vicar came back yesterday with his entourage; he will be staying a little longer, perhaps until the new year. Since Robert found out he was coming, he has seemed worried, and I have gathered that two visits so close together mean that his management of the abbey is in question, that the powers that be want to keep a closer eye on him or collect evidence against him.

I was summoned to the abbot's apartments after sext. A cheering fire was burning, and a mixture of hay and aromatic herbs had been spread on the ground and crackled underfoot. The vicar was seated at his desk when I entered, and he motioned for me to sit in front of him.

'I believe you know the Baron of Bourraches.'

I don't know how he had found out, but it was true that I had eaten at his table when I was working in the atelier. He had prepared a banquet for everyone who had contributed to a huge painting of him with his wife and dogs, a considerable affair that had kept us busy for weeks. He was a man who laughed loudly, talked loudly and ate for two. I nodded my head.

'Perhaps you know that he is a close friend of the abbot.'

I didn't know. Cautiously, I stayed silent. He went on.

'The Baron has a wife who is both virtuous and fertile and who has given him four children.'

I remembered. She was a creature with a long face, unfortunate features and extremely white hands. I had painted her fingers.

'But for some time the Baron has also had a young protégée, the niece of a friend, who is particularly dear to him. We would like to give him a portrait of this young woman. Can we count on you?'

It wasn't really a question. And why all of a sudden was he referring to 'we'?

'Alas, I am afraid not.'

He grabbed a carafe of wine, filled two goblets and set one before me. The spiced liquid warmed my throat. After months of the watered-down, inferior wine served at the refectory, I practically had tears in my eyes. The vicar was smiling like a man who understands your worries, sympathizes and can do nothing about them.

'I have asked around about you,' he told me as if it were a favour, 'and I know that you haven't handled a brush in a long time, but I also know that you were a talented portrait artist. Would this not be the perfect opportunity to take up your art again?'

'I don't think so.'

'Of course you would be paid for your work. Handsomely.'

'I hardly need money anymore,' I pointed out.

'Yes, it seems you have embraced the monastic life… Well, not entirely. Routine and silence are wonderful refuges for a distraught mind. But surely you know that your presence here is against the rules. You have not taken your vows and apparently have no desire to do so; you are not a guest of the abbot, but of your friend Robert, whose schemes, you should know, are raising questions in high places… I am sure you do not want to add to his worries… Take a few days to think about it. We'll talk again the day after tomorrow,' he said, and he thanked me.

I left the room. It was raining outside, drops as grey as the stone.

I had never seen the young person named Gertrude. To create her likeness, the vicar expected me to use a miniature portrait and a letter that described her. He also provided the colours and brushes, down to the wood panel I was to paint on. He had never doubted that I would accept.

The letter said that the young lady was a great beauty, blond, with a long neck, a high forehead and limpid eyes. On the miniature what I saw instead was a rather plain face framed with brown hair. The neck was not visible, and the eyes appeared to be brown, although the letter said they were blue. The missive and the painting seemed to present two different people, but that was no surprise: the first provided insight into the person who wrote it, the second into the person who painted it. When we think we are speaking about others, we are always speaking about ourselves, and whoever thinks they are painting the portrait of a church or an apple finds themselves drawing their own face on the page.

Both in the description and in the little painting, Gertrude seemed pretty but vapid – in a way worse than ugly: empty. She was no doubt perfect for the Baron, who liked to fill his stomach with wine and sausages. Her an empty jug, him a full wineskin.

One should not pass judgment on the subjects of one's paintings, I know this. It shows in the portrait. Robert would say that it is only up to God in his infinite wisdom to judge. But I couldn't help myself; all of her features reminded me that she is not Anna, and that was her crime.

I finished the portrait in a few days. It was neither good nor bad. My fingers took to the brush as if they had never put it down. Accustomed to the halting movements of the quill, I am almost ashamed to say I enjoyed feeling the silk slide over the smooth wood. Even the smell of the pastes was familiar; it was the reds, blues and yellows of the life I had left behind.

In the kitchens where I went to get the water and vinegar I needed, they were busy with Christmas dinner: rabbit, guinea fowl, geese, suckling pig, capons and pike had been neatly decapitated, dismembered and cut up. Heads, torsos, feet, fins and tails were lined up on the large wooden table, waiting to be reassembled into new creatures. This delicate task was reserved for Brother Gaspard, who was responsible for the abbey's meals. While the monks took turns every week in the kitchens to prepare the communal meals, for years Brother Gaspard had been exclusively assigned to the service of the abbey's superior and his guests, who required special attention.

Around him, assistants kneaded dough and prepared broths according to his instructions. The room smelled of butter, thyme, cloves and nutmeg. The flames roared in the huge fireplaces where poultry was hung to roast on a spit, necks crammed against butts. From time to time, a drop trickled down the birds that were glistening with fat, dropping into the fire to disappear with a sizzle.

Brother Gaspard had carefully taken the head of the suckling pig and placed it on the body of the capon. It fit perfectly, but that was the problem: there was not enough contrast. A question of proportions. The two of them could have been cousins. He set down the poultry, then took the cold body of the large fish instead, adjusting the head, pulling a bit in front and in back, as if trying on a hat. He smiled, and it seemed as though the suckling pig returned his smile as he took a needle and thread to delicately sew the fish-pig, groin open, fins splayed.

§

For the first time that Christmas night, the monks celebrated vespers in the new church, which was still only half-finished. The wall raised after the collapse of the choir's ceiling, which for years had separated it from the nave, was torn down, and you could see the entire space when you walked through the door, which we did ceremoniously, in a long line. It took my breath away: it was like entering a forest of stone. Majestic pillars rose up, alternating with breaks of sky where the stained glass would be fitted. For the time being, even though when you looked up you could see the first blond planks of the new ceiling that will be like an upside-down ship's hull, you still got the impression of being half-outdoors. A voice rose up:

'In nomine Patris, et Filii, et Spiritus Sancti.'

To which the others murmured in unison, *'Amen.'*

The words were quickly carried off by the winds of the bay.

Exceptionally, a few workers were attending the service, among them the recent foreman, a tall, thin man who knew the responses and said them with the monks. His men sat in the back and remained silent. There were barely twenty of them, but they still outnumbered the monks, who seemed dwarfed by the immense vault. All of a sudden, the men and the stones no longer seemed as solid; both were crumbling, straightening up and falling, just to get back up again.

§

The vicar seemed to like the painting I brought him. He wanted to give me a handful of coins, but I refused, saying that Robert would undoubtedly know better than me how to put them to the abbey's use. He looked angry and returned the pieces of silver to his purse without a word.

I saw him again only at the evening meal, where a lavish table had been set. He politely admired the tray on which the hybrids assembled by Brother Gaspard were laid, reminiscent of the mythical creatures in the margins of the books in the library. It is astonishing that monasteries devoted to God and divine knowledge harbour so many monsters within their books and on their plates.

Nearby, Brother Maximilien pursed his lips. He refused to touch the creations, aberrations of nature, because if the Lord in His infinite wisdom had wanted men to eat capons with the heads of rabbits and carps with pheasants' tails, He would have put them in the lakes and the farmyards, as he explained to Robert, taking a handful of grapes.

After the meal, the vicar had us go into what he was using as a sitting room. The fire was already lit, seats had been set out around it. Brother Louis sat down as soon as we were invited to do so: Brother Clément and Robert remained standing. I did likewise. The vicar had taken his seat at the same time as Brother Maximilien, and seeing that he would have to lift his eyes to speak to us, quickly stood back up and started to pace between the hearth and the door.

'Your abbey is magnificent,' he began. 'People say it is a wonder, but it is even more beautiful than that.'

Brother Louis could only agree. 'Our library is still one of the most important in all of Christendom,' he said, and you could feel that the *still* burned his lips.

'Of course, but I wanted to talk about your gardens,' the vicar continued in an even tone.

Brother Louis bristled; Brother Clément appeared not to have heard. Robert stared at the fire.

'But in fact we were wondering,' the vicar went on with the tone of a man who wonders about nothing because he already knows the answer to the question he is pretending to ask, 'if it would not be better to transfer some of your more valuable books to the library at the Abbey of Saint Ouen, in Rouen.'

Brother Louis flinched as if a wasp had stung him. The goblet of wine he was holding started to tremble. So that's what was in the works. I would have liked to have grabbed the portrait I had just given this hypocrite and thrown it on the fire. Robert did not turn around.

'The Abbey of Saint Ouen would be better able to protect them,' the vicar continued. 'And they have monks who are still young, who understand Greek, who have a steady hand and a sharp eye. And correct me if I am wrong, but you lost half of the books in the collapse of the north tower of the church, and the abbey barely escaped being occupied by the English a few years ago.'

'And we defended it honourably!' Brother Maximilien said, having set his goblet on a table. 'Not a single book left these walls! And not a single Englishman entered them!'

'Of course,' the vicar agreed. 'But who will protect fragile books from fire, for example? Hasn't your bell tower been hit by lightning several times, the last time just a few weeks ago? Who can say when lightning will strike again? Or the plague?'

He crossed himself upon saying that word.

I looked at Robert, who was still not moving, in front of the fire. I was still waiting for him to intervene vociferously to protect the library he had devoted his life to, but he remained silent.

'Our books must remain here,' Brother Louis continued, his voice choked with emotion.

'*Your* books?' the vicar asked.

'They were copied here, by monks who are resting in peace under this earth, or they were given as gifts to the abbey by travellers who deemed us fit to protect them. If they are not ours, surely they belong to the archangel Michel,' he answered, sending a desperate glance Robert's way, urging him to intervene. But Robert was staying stubbornly silent.

'The books belong to God,' the vicar continued in an even voice, 'whether here or at Saint Ouen. The matter has been settled,' he added. 'Tomorrow I will make an initial selection.'

Leaning out the window of the scriptorium, Brother Louis stared at the dark waters of the bay under the sky dotted with tiny, twinkling stars.

There, two centuries earlier, some one hundred volumes had foundered at the same time as the tower that housed them when it collapsed in the middle of the night. Over the weeks that followed, a few were found, brought in by the tide. The pages were bleached like whale skeletons, scoured by the salt. The others never reappeared; they had been swallowed by oblivion, quicksand, giant octopuses.

One of those books was the library's catalogue. So it was never known exactly which books had been lost, or just how many had disappeared. Some remembered a book having been on the shelves that others maintained had been lent to a foreign abbey or returned to its owners. Books that had not been consulted for years had been engulfed without anyone noticing: they were already dead before they drowned. Some remembered books that could not have existed and that they must have read in their dreams.

Brother Louis had got his hands on a heavy volume by Plutarch that he had recopied himself more than twenty years before. The copy that had served as the model had since disappeared. Another had been lost in the fire at the Abbey of Gembloux, some three centuries earlier. To his knowledge, there was no longer a full copy of *Parallel Lives* in existence. He ran his thumb over the kidskin cover, opened the book at random and read a sentence in a low voice, as one would say a prayer. It was the epitaph of Scipio, whose life mirrored that of Epaminondas.

'Ungrateful fatherland, you will not have my bones.'

He leaned out the window into the cold air, folded his torso over the stone. And then, like a mad sower, he threw the book into the waves among the flickering stars.

There was a ghost library in the grey water at the base of the rock. No one could steal that one from him.

December 24, four in the afternoon. People are bustling in the lobby of the inn, laying the table with biscuits, spiced wine and hot chocolate. My daughter is still sleeping, which explains how I can be here, beside the fire, sipping tea perfumed with flowers. But I will not associate this book (which is not yet a book) with a tea, a fragrance or a place. I am writing it on the sly, as her naps and my short breaks allow. I have said that I write to lose myself – it's true – but I am also writing this book (which may never be a book) to find myself again. To find the person who knows how to write behind the one who soothes, rocks, feeds, cajoles, sings, reassures, nourishes and heals. This book is a room of my own.

§

A while ago, looking at a comet in a book, my daughter pointed to its golden tail and said, 'Hair.' This is the same analogy that Michel Tournier makes in *Gaspard, Melchior et Balthazar*, the first part of which deals with blondness, and Christ, one of its supposed incarnations. *Comet*, from the Greek *kometes*: *long-haired*. Learning and discovering the language, my little girl reinvents it, and yet it's the same.

Noël, *dies natalis*, day of birth in the darkest of winter: a point that shines in the night.

An apocryphal etymology has it that the word *Noël* comes rather from the French word *nouvelle*, for *story*, and while untrue, this explanation is pleasing – anywhere we find stories we are in a friendly territory. At the same time I learn that the term *Yule log* has not always designated the cake, but that it used to be an actual log, which was placed in the hearth at sundown and was to burn the whole night through. My story, my Christmas story, will be the same: it will provide warmth until sunrise.

§

Richly illuminated, a book of hours from the Middle Ages was intended for laypeople to follow the Liturgy of the Hours, the different services that punctuated the day and the night. This sort of book is cruelly missing from our era: a sort of *vade mecum* to constantly remind us how to live not happily but peacefully.

Anyone who has become a mother – or perhaps a parent – has experienced that fundamental and irreversible shift: suddenly one day, we are moved from the centre of the universe to the sidelines. I have to relearn everything, as if I too had just come into the world: how to eat, sleep, be completely fused with another being and little by little let go. There are no more days or nights, just an expanse of time punctuated by feedings. During the first weeks, like clockwork, my daughter would wake up two or three times in the middle of the night (matin, lauds), I would pick her up out of her crib, and we would sit together in a velvet armchair in the corner of the room. The house would sleep. Through the window, the leafless maple kept watch, the silver dome of Vincent-d'Indy music school gleaming in the dark like a big moon. Often it would snow. We could hear the wind whistling through the branches.

When we arrive in Boston, the first thing I look for and find in the apartment is a velvet armchair near a window. It is in the front bedroom; we sleep in the one at the back of the house. Two or three times a night (matin, lauds), my daughter wakes up, I pick her up, and I bring the turtle nightlight with us to avoid having to turn on a light. On the walls and the ceiling, the stars and the moon jump and twirl to the rhythm of my steps, falling still as we settle into the armchair. The heavy curtain is drawn to keep the cold air out. My daughter feeds, and I dream of my maple.

For months, I don't write a line. Little by little, as if I were learning to talk again, I regain my ability to describe ducks, trees, the sea, from the simplest to the grandest. One day, I even manage to read: *Les désarçonnés*, by Pascal Quignard, the story of men and women who fall off horses and whose broken lives are rebuilt, one piece at a time. First I read a paragraph a day, then an entire page. I still haven't reached the end.

§

I am trying to see the colours on Éloi's palette as he saw them.

Originally the word *miniature* didn't mean a drawing or ornamentation, but a colour: red. The term comes from the Latin *miniare, to paint with minium, red, cinnabar*. Through a metonymic process, the content has come to designate the container. Plus, *red* originally meant *root*, whereas *brown* originally meant *dark*. *Blue* comes from the Old French *blo*, which means *pale*. Before the Late Middle Ages, there was no word to designate blue in European languages. It was considered a shade of white, black or green, depending on whether it was light blue, dark blue or aqua blue. That a thousand years ago they couldn't name purple, orange or pink seems conceivable; these are complex hues not commonly found in nature. But that they did not have a name for one of the three primary colours, the one we now associate with the sky and the water, is astonishing. People at the time lived under a black sky and fished white fish from a green sea – or they lived under a green sky and fished black fish from a white sea.

§

My daughter, to whom I have just explained wishing people good things for the New Year, wished for me light, a wardrobe and a tree. And bars. When she said that, she was looking at the bars at the head of the metal bed where we were lying to read stories – but still.

Bars aside, the light and the tree are no doubt the most beautiful wishes anyone has ever wished for me. I hope they come true.

Within these walls, I ended up finding not peace or even relief, which is a more modest form of peace, but a sort of calm, as if I had turned half to stone. I had observed this phenomenon when I was painting portraits: men naturally take on the features that surround them. A seigneur who loves hunting will have the quivering nostrils of his dogs, whereas you can see the blood flowing in the veins under the skin of a barber surgeon. Birds of a feather flock together, so there is a risk to keeping company with the idiotic and the evil.

But I think that this calm also comes from a plant that Brother Clément gave me a few weeks ago as I was walking aimlessly down the rows of the herbularius.

Busy pruning a bush, he nodded at me as I walked near him, and then bent over to take a square of white linen from his basket, which contained a brownish powder and small dried white flowers.

'A pinch in warm water before going to bed,' was all he said.

The handkerchief gave off a foul smell.

'The smell alone is enough to chase away bad dreams,' he added, smiling.

Since that day, I have stopped having nightmares. But I've also stopped seeing her in my dreams, and her memory is slowly fading from my mind just as her flesh is dissolving into the ground.

§

Twice a day, Mont Saint-Michel becomes an island. The rest of the time, it is a piece of land precariously attached to the rest of the continent, as if its mission were to remind us that ties are fragile, ephemeral. We are never as alone or as surrounded as we care to believe. This struck me one day as I was coming back from a longer walk than usual.

As you approach, the village and the abbey seem like a single creature in stone. I don't know why, but every time I look at them from the bay, I think of a snail. There is only one actual road in the village that slopes and leads to the abbey; the rest are just alleys and passageways, no wider than a man, running between the houses, like secret tunnels. For the most part, the inhabitants engage in trade with the pilgrims, offering them trinkets or room and board. And the monks up above trade only with God.

That morning at low tide, I left by the King's Gate, and I walked until the abbey looked quite small, like a sand-castle. This sort of thing used to fascinate me: the way objects grow smaller as you move away from them, how two straight lines that are long enough become oblique and seem to meet up on the horizon. Out of a sense of duty, from time to time I would go out around town, stop pretty much anywhere and force myself to draw what was there, not what I thought I saw. Sometimes I would draw these sketches with a single line, without dropping my eyes to the page. When I had had enough of these exercises, I would draw the birds.

On the sand of the bay, a man was fishing for cockles with his daughter. Both had short rakes and regular, precise gestures. She was young, practically a child, but she may as well have been there for centuries, bent over looking for shells buried in the sand. She didn't look like Anna: tall and thin, she had hair like straw and the tanned skin of someone who went out in the sun regularly. She raised her head toward me and smiled. I froze, as if she had spoken to me in a foreign language. I walked faster. But the young girl's smile – the young woman's smile – stayed with me: it was the first I had seen in months.

On my return, I took off my boots to feel the cold sand

under my feet. It seemed as though I could feel each minuscule grain between my toes. Seagulls circled in the sky. The entire bay was suddenly alive.

I hurried because soon the sea was going to rise, and Robert had warned me a hundred times that the tides take Mont Saint-Michel by storm faster than a galloping horse. But a short way from the walls, I spotted a small form bent over the ground straightening up and starting to run in the direction of the sea. He seemed to be chasing something white that had flown away.

I yelled out, 'Be careful! Come back!'

He was too far away and didn't hear me, or chose to ignore me and kept running, then froze and bent over the sand once again. I saw the water sparkling in the distance. The tide would be coming in soon. I started running toward the child, whom I recognized: it was the little sick boy's friend, who had spent most of his days at Casimir's bedside.

I yelled again, this time calling him by name. 'Andreas! Hurry back!'

He ignored me again. I felt as though I could almost hear the hiss of the waves that kept advancing and would quickly surround Mont Saint-Michel. And on top of it all, the child was at a spot where a man had been killed a few weeks earlier and where we would see pilgrims get stuck in the mud every month. Sometimes it took hours to get them out of the silt that closed in around them, and we often had to dispatch one of the brothers to guide them through the labyrinth of quicksand that surrounds the abbey.

When I reached Andreas, he was clutching a bunch of crinkled pages to his chest, on which you could still make out the lines drawn in black ink.

'Come on, we have to go back!' I said, grabbing him by the elbow.

But he got away and was off again, running straight out to the open sea. He headed into the water up to his thighs to try to grab another page floating on the surface. I followed him, stumbling in the icy sea. The water was murky, and you couldn't see the bottom, which was not even a toise below; I lost my footing, wound up on my hands and knees in the water, my mouth full of sand and salt. Getting up, I recovered my balance and managed to grab him again to pull him toward me. This time, he let himself be dragged along.

Still clutching the sheets to his chest, he broke into a wide smile and told me, 'I found a treasure.'

§

'A library, you see,' Robert was trying to explain to Brother Clément this afternoon, 'is also a garden: if you stop caring for it, it dies.'

I think that was the longest conversation he had ever had with the gardener. Could he even understand such an image? No doubt wanting to give him something that was more within his grasp, Robert said, 'Books exist only as long as they are read and recopied, going on to continue their lives elsewhere, like flowers that spread their petals.'

Clément smiled. 'Actually, when flowers lose their petals, their life is coming to an end. They sow their seeds into the wind to reproduce. But I understand your meaning.'

Robert blushed. Thinking he was addressing an idiot, he had made an idiot of himself. But Clément's voice was in no way mocking.

The three of us were in the garden. Robert was in the habit of going to collect his thoughts in the underground church or on the tomb of Robert de Torigni, with whom he shared a name, but that day he didn't seem to have found any comfort there, and his feet had led him to the herbularius, where I had come in search of an infusion for the sick little boy. The grey cat had greeted him, meowing. Clément was using a mortar to crush herbs that would be used as a remedy.

Robert continued, as if for his own benefit, 'The library is the heart of the abbey; without it, Mont Saint-Michel would barely be more than a cemetery where pilgrims come to see the skull of Aubert and touch the imprint of the foot of Michael, both dead as stone. It is not enough to keep the books that we have managed to save from past centuries carefully locked up; we need new books and, for that, new scribes with a love of wisdom and an indifference to the noise of the world. But now monks and artists have flooded the cities. There are countless clerics in the universities. The abbeys are slowly sinking into oblivion, and our library has been dying the death of a thousand small cuts for centuries.'

'It has been dying for so long, it is practically immortal,' Clément replied, still smiling.

Robert didn't answer. They were silent for a moment. Clément continued to crush the herbs and the flowers. The cat was rolling on its back nearby. How was it always so clean when it wallowed in filth? I was looking above at the mass of stone built to protect men whose mission it was to protect books. The endless arrogance of this suddenly hit me: it wasn't the books that needed the monks' protection – it was the men who needed the books. We will die. The books will survive.

Robert sat beside Brother Clément and took a pinch of powder, which he brought to his nose. His eyes on the ground, Clément asked him, 'Are you in a great deal of pain?'

Robert gave a start and glanced at me. Then he whispered, 'Some days.' He smiled weakly. 'Hemlock dulls it a little.'

Clément nodded his head. 'I've said nothing to the vicar or his aides, assuming that that was your wish,' he finally said.

Robert thanked him with a nod of his chin. My throat was knotted, and I cleared it but still couldn't manage a word. At that moment, my friend was like the few winter flowers that surrounded him: forsaken, fragile and stubborn.

§

One evening before vespers, he accompanied me to the sick little boy's bedside. Andreas was already sitting there, along with Clément, who had come to give him his potion for the evening. We joined him in silence. Andreas looked at Robert with curiosity, hesitated a moment and then asked, 'Are you the one who keeps the books?'

Robert smiled at him. 'If you will.'

The child pulled the bundle he had saved from the bay from behind his back. The sheets had dried, but even to my eyes it was clear that half of the text had been lost.

'I found these.'

Robert furrowed his brow, held out his hand and examined the pages Andreas was holding out to him.

'Where did you find these?'

'In the sand.'

'Where in the sand?'

'Near the walls.'

I gestured with my head to indicate that it was true. I could see Robert trying to recognize the text. He seemed to give up.

'Were there more?' he finally asked.

'Oh, yes!' the child replied. 'But I couldn't get them all. The tide took them.'

Robert smoothed the sheets as if he were petting a familiar animal, then handed the bundle back to the child, saying, 'These are yours. You saved them. Take care of them now.'

The child hugged the sheets to his chest, and then asked, 'Is it true that they are all different?'

Robert raised his eyebrows. Distractedly following their conversation, I was watching Casimir, who was lying there, breathing lightly. Clément's eyes went from Robert to the boy sitting before him. He seemed quite interested in their discussion.

'Books,' the child continued. 'Are they all different?'

'Yes and no,' Robert answered. 'There are hundreds of different books, written since antiquity, but there are no doubt dozens of copies of some of them.'

'They were transcribed by dozens of people at once?'

'No, not at once,' Robert said, smiling, 'but copied and recopied in different places over the years, so that now there may be copies of this book in Moscow or Constantinople. Or you may have the only one.'

The child was silent for a moment. No doubt he had heard the word *Constantinople* before, the syllables bringing to mind wars and Our Lord's tomb.

'But,' the child continued, 'they are not all exactly alike if they have been copied by different people at different times, right?'

I smiled. I had had the same thought. This time, it was Clément who answered him. 'What really makes them not all alike,' he said softly, 'is that they are read by different people at different times.'

The child seemed astonished, but not as much as Robert.

When we got up to leave a few minutes later, Clément got up too. Our sandals reverberated on the cold stone. A wind blew in from the sea, forcing us to tuck our hands into our coats and walk with our chins down. And yet Clément led us in the direction of the cloister, where we continued to walk, talking in low voices.

'Did you hear about that man in Germany who has figured out how to copy the same book one hundred times?' he asked.

Robert smiled. 'So is he eternal?"

'He may well be.' Clément also smiled, to contradict the meaning of his words.

'If what you say is true,' Robert said, 'then he will truly be eternal, because his name will still be known in one thousand years.'

'I know his name today: Johannes Gutenberg. He is a simple goldsmith.'

'People have always been given to flights of fancy,' Robert said. 'Someone will claim that he has created a flying machine, someone else a device for walking to the bottom of the sea. Silliness. Why would this Gutenberg be any different?'

'Because he has already succeeded in doing what he says.'

'And how can you be so sure of that?' I asked.

'I have seen his books.'

I was speechless. So was Robert. I thought that nothing more from the curious gardener could surprise him, but if Brother Clément himself had invented this incredible process, Robert couldn't have been more astonished.

'I have held in my own hands two *Ars minor* by Donatus that he printed, perfectly alike,' Clément explained. 'The same book twice.'

'And how did he do this?'

'Using a machine that looks a bit like a wine press. He puts a metal plate covered with ink on it where the text to be reproduced is engraved. Then he just puts a piece of paper on it to print the text.'

The explanation was clear, the process disarmingly simple. When I closed my eyes, I could almost see the machine. I was sure Clément was telling the truth.

'But,' I asked, driven by curiosity, 'it must take months to engrave the plates, one at a time. It must take even longer than giving the book to a scribe.'

'I expressed myself poorly,' Clément continued. 'The text is not engraved on it: it is made using characters than can be picked up and moved wherever you want, so that a single set of letters allows you to make any book.'

Suddenly the invention became quite simply incredible: all books were contained in a pile of characters – every book ever written, and all those yet to be written, lying together, jumbled up, under the fingers of this man, this German man.

Robert looked blindly into the darkness ahead of him. I imagine he was trying to decide whether this news foretold the death of the library or its rebirth. How do you live in a world where books can be made without men? He would never get to find out. Maybe it was better that way.

'And how many of these grammar books are in existence?' he asked, as he would have asked someone who had seen a unicorn the number of legs it had. The answer could be ten or one thousand; it was of no importance.

'I don't know,' Clément answered. 'I just have the one.'

I thought I had misunderstood him. Then I told myself that Brother Clément had again expressed himself poorly.

'You have seen only one?' Robert asked.

'I have seen two,' Brother Clément went on, patiently, 'but I have just one. Would you like to see it?'

In his cabin in the middle of the vegetable garden, in the midst of the pots, shovels and seeds, Clément had a hidden library: twelve works stored in a wooden chest, wrapped in a sheet of linen.

He held out to Robert a small, ordinary-looking book. It was Donatus's grammar book. *One* of the grammar books. Robert looked at it, stupefied, and handed it to me. The pages were cool to my touch, the characters perfectly uniform. Closing my eyes, I felt as though I could have made them out just by touch. I opened my eyes and the impression passed. Robert was trembling beside me. The ground had started to spin beneath our feet. This book was a monster. It was a marvel.

That was the real fire.

The child stayed pretty much unconscious, wracked with fever, for another week. Andreas ended up leaving too, taking his book with him, but leaving the pilgrim's shell for his friend. What he was returning to, no doubt he didn't even know, but he had to get walking.

I spent my days and nights at the young patient's bedside; I fed him chicken broth and put cold compresses on his forehead. Brother Clément came three times a day with a steaming cup with bitter-smelling herbs floating in it. He would lift Casimir gently and have him drink the brew, and, without saying a word, return to take care of his plants. Sometimes his cat would come with him and curl up at the little boy's feet, purring. In the hours afterward, the patient was less agitated in his sleep, and sometimes I managed to close my eyes for more than a few minutes. When the child quieted down, the cat would leave silently.

One evening, after Brother Clément had just come in, the cat on his heels, Brother Gontier showed up with a bowl and a knife.

'What are you planning to do, my brother?' Clément asked in a respectful tone.

'This child will not get better until we have driven out the humours that are polluting his blood,' Gontier said, as he kneeled by the bed.

The cat, which had lain down, now stood, but didn't leave. It simply turned its head toward its master, eyes half-shut.

Moving in unison, Clément and I stood between the blade and the child.

'You are too kind to concern yourself with his health when you have so much to do,' Clément said. 'But I am sure that more important duties are calling.' He did not move an inch as he said the words.

'I know you claim to be able to heal him with your herbs,' Gontier replied, looking at the bowl with the remains of golden liquid, 'but it is time to give him a real remedy, one that will get at the cause of his illness.'

'He's sleeping,' Clément continued. "Isn't it better to let him rest?'

'He will sleep better afterward,' Gontier replied, trying to get past him.

The gardener was as still as a rock.

'Ah! Will you leave me to it?' Gontier exclaimed, furious, and the cat responded by hissing.

'I'm afraid not,' Brother Clément continued calmly.

I smiled. Brother Gontier stamped his foot, flew into a rage, swore he would tell Robert about this lack of respect, and ended up leaving with an empty bowl and a pristine knife in his hand. Casimir kept sleeping, breathing in small bursts. He had pulled off the sheepskin that had been laid over him. I pulled it up his chest, which was rising and falling in time with his fitful breath.

Brother Clément left after squeezing my arm, as if entrusting me with the little patient. The cat curled back into a ball at the child's feet. I sat at his side on the cold stone and picked up a handful of blades on the ground that had escaped from his straw mattress, twirled them around in my fingers before starting to braid them. All this time, I didn't take my eyes off the thin face. You could see his eyes move from left to right under his thin eyelids. The child was dreaming like a small dog, complete with starts and jerks.

I bent and smoothed the straw between my palms, knotted it, braided stray pieces, squeezed the stalks until they were in the shape of a golden bird with pointy wings and set this near the child's head, between his neck and his cheek.

Its presence seemed to calm him; his breathing slowed, he inhaled more deeply.

He was still dreaming, but in his dreams he had flown away.

§

One morning, he opened his eyes and saw what was around him. The next day, he ate on his own. The day after that, he wanted to get up.

That morning, for the first time since Anna's death, I picked up a piece of charcoal. The stick that had once been a young willow was now light as a feather between my fingers. In the centre, you could make out the first tree's growth circles, which were darker. Even black has its own black.

Letting my hand guide me, I sketched the slate roofs of the houses that could be seen from the cell where the little boy was resting. I made them dark or pale by pressing harder or softer on the tip, using my thumb to blend the hard edges. I wasn't thinking about what I was doing – my fingers knew what to do. The child watched my gestures, intrigued. His eyes moved from the slate gables to the sheet of paper as if to make sure he wasn't mistaken. And when he saw the contour of the house of the Chevalier du Guesclin appear below, he burst out laughing.

It was just a rough sketch, done in no time and with no colour, but the child was already looking at it as if it held something magic. And then I drew a piece of slate in a longer, more rounded shape. I stuck wings on it, a fanned tail and a pointy beak. I gave another fins and a thick-lipped mouth. To draw the portrait of a fish, start by drawing a roof, then a bird.

Now the slates were taking flight from the roofs of the little houses, rising like fireworks into the sky or plunging into the bay. The child's eyes gleamed with the reflection of the creatures invented for him. Anna was right when she insisted on embroidering her sea serpents and unicorns. In the space of a second, I found her again, at the same time as a reason to work: to show what doesn't exist. We only ever give what we are missing.

We stayed hunched over the drawing for a long time. The child was watching the stone turned into a bird, and I was watching him watch. Of the two, I had the better view.

On Friday, March 20, 2015, at daybreak, Mont Saint-Michel became an island again. The photos show water engulfing part of the causeway. Small silhouettes are gathered on it, waiting for who knows what. The phenomenon is due to the equinox tides, particularly strong this spring. The water will withdraw during the day and then, this evening, what was once Mont Tombe will be returned to the sea.

I hadn't seen it for over five years. The last time we went to Normandy, I avoided it. My excuses were no better or worse than those from the last time: my daughter and I had been sick; I was exhausted; we were in a hurry to get back to Paris. Since then, it is as though I have been feeling around for it in books, on paper, in my memories, some of which are so distant and vague that I no longer know whether they are mine.

I found it only this morning. It was standing in the middle of the water, in peril of the sea.

Acknowledgments

The author: Thanks to Nadine Bismuth and Éric Fontaine, who read the first draft of the manuscript. Thanks to Antoine Tanguay, who made it a book. Thanks to François Ricard, without whom this book would have been altogether different. Thanks to Alana Wilcox, at Coach House Books, who gave Éloi a second life, and to Rhonda Mullins, who gave him his English voice.

The translator: Thanks to Alana Wilcox and everyone at Coach House Books for bringing such wonderful French-language books to English audiences. Thanks to Dominique Fortier for allowing me to fall under the spell of her writing.

Dominique Fortier was born in Quebec City. After receiving a doctorate in French literature from McGill University, she began working as an editor, translator and publisher. Her first novel, *Du bon usage des étoiles* (2008), was a finalist for the Governor General's Literary Award and won the Prix Gens de mer at the Saint-Malo Étonnants Voyageurs film and literary festival. It was translated into English as *On the Proper Use of Stars*. She is also the author of *Les larmes de saint Laurent* (translated as *Wonder*), *La porte du ciel* and, with Nicolas Dickner, *Révolutions*. She lives in Outremont, Quebec.

Rhonda Mullins is a writer and translator living in Montreal. She won the 2015 Governor General's Literary Award for Translation for Jocelyne Saucier's *Twenty-One Cardinals*. *And the Birds Rained Down*, her translation of Saucier's *Il pleuvait des oiseaux*, was a CBC Canada Reads Selection for 2015. It was also shortlisted for the Governor General's Literary Award, as were her translations of Élise Turcotte's *Guyana* and Hervé Fischer's *The Decline of the Hollywood Empire*.

Typeset in Baskerville

Printed at the Coach House on bpNichol Lane in Toronto, Ontario, on Zephyr Antique Laid paper, which was manufactured, acid-free, in Saint-Jérôme, Quebec, from second-growth forests. This book was printed with vegetable-based ink on a 1965 Heidelberg KORD offset litho press. Its pages were folded on a Baumfolder, gathered by hand, bound on a Sulby Auto-Minabinda and trimmed on a Polar single-knife cutter.

Edited and designed by Alana Wilcox
Cover design by Ingrid Paulson
Cover images: detail from *Profile Portrait of a Young Lady* by
    Antonio del Pollaiuolo, detail from a postcard of Mont
    Saint-Michel on Wikipédia
Photo of Dominique Fortier by Julie Artacho
Photo of Rhonda Mullins by Owen Egan

Coach House Books
80 bpNichol Lane
Toronto ON M5S 3J4
Canada

416 979 2217
800 367 6360

mail@chbooks.com
www.chbooks.com